THE SEER, THE SENTINEL, THE SEEKER AND THE ORBS

J. L. Coates

Other books by the author

Writing as Judith Coates

Be Who You Be
Let Your Light Shine

Writing as J. L. Coates

Second Chances
Awakening
Tw Women, Two Loves, Two Stories
Shattered: A Family in Crisis

Library and Archives Canada Cataloguing in Publication J. L. Coates

Judy Coates: E-mail jcoates@telusplanet.net

ISBN   978-0-9880735-8-6

Cover by Google images
Printed in USA by Createspace

For my mentor, teacher and editor **Dianne Tchir.** Without your support and encouragement my dream of becoming a writer would never have come true. You believed in me, which in turn helped me believe in myself.
Thank you for everything.

The names, places and events in this story are fictional and the result of my over-active imagination. Any similarities to real people, places and situations are coincidental.

Table of Contents

PRELUDE

Since the beginning of time the mighty God of Creation, Eros, determined the world would be populated with three types of people: the Seers, the Sentinels, and the lay people or the general population.

The Seers were a select group of women who had the ability to foretell the future. They didn't have the ability to change what was going to happen, but could tell what the effect of an action would be.

This sometimes unwanted gift was passed down to the first born daughters of each successive generation. Because of this, they were always in danger. There would always be those who would wish to control the activities of the Seer for their own benefit.

As soon as Eros granted women the right to be Seers he realized that they, and their daughters required special protection, therefore he created the warrior Sentinels. Only the first born son of a Sentinel could have this post, and their sworn duty from birth to death was to protect the Seer they were assigned to. Many times the life of a Seer, and the ability to perform her duties would depend upon his protection.

From a very young age all of the men created by Eros were taught the skills needed to be a warrior. Although the role of Sentinel was preordained for a select few, he was not called upon until needed.

Eros formed four orbs representing the mighty forces of the heavens: Earth, Wind, Fire, and Water. The orb representing the earth was at the center, the balance. The other three were the forces of change which could alter the balance. He gave the Seers the power to use the orbs as a way of communicating between the people and the Gods. The smaller ones were used daily by the Seers and the fourth, a larger orb sat in the center of a jewel encrusted case. The full power of the orbs was only effective when all were together in one place – the Seer and the orbs. The Gods were all seeing, all knowing, and used the orbs as a way to maintain peace and harmony. After each use, the orbs were hidden in a secret location known only to Eros.

Any man, who came into the possession of the four orbs and the Seer, would have the ability to rule the world. Unless he had all together, in one place, the power was lost.

Eros built a beautiful palace in the hills of Delphi overlooking the deep blue water of the Delphian Sea. Tall white marble columns tipped with gold, soared into the bright blue sky. Beautiful fountains and gardens surrounded the columns, and had been built in such a way that the evening sun, reflecting off on the golden tips of the columns, cast their glow onto the fountain pools and gardens below.

In the middle of this vast complex stood a circular building surrounded by pure gold columns, its center opened to the air. A small area, covered with a red tile roof, contained the room of the Oracle of Delphi. At specific times of the day, the young women chosen to be Seers rotated as councilors to the people. For a price, every citizen was able to consult with the Oracle and receive an answer to their question.

The ceremony was very specific. The Oracle was led to her seat by a palace guard, who assisted her to sit on a triangular shaped chair located above a fissure in the earth, from which a sweet fume was emitted. Her white gown was artfully draped around her, and flowers decorated her hair. She would sit with her eyes closed, with one of the glass orbs resting in her hands. The jewel encrusted case containing the rest of the orbs sat on a high, black, polished rock behind her.

Visitors, both rich and poor, walked up a path known as the Sacred Way to pay their homage to the Oracle. They prayed as they walked, and once at the top made a donation to the temple, according to their station in life. The wealthy were expected to give gold, the others, whatever they could afford. Specific gifts were given for answers to specific questions such as, "will I conceive a child?"

As each person approached the oracle he kneeled down, bowed his head, and asked his question. The oracle would open her eyes, look into the orb and give him an answer. As always, the answer was left to the interpretation of the visitor. The slightest variation in the question often produced a different answer.

There were few rules which governed the Seers and Sentinels alike but, what there were was of vital importance.

First rule: After ten years of service the Seers were allowed to leave their role of Oracle and marry this insured that their line would carry on in the future. At an early age the first born daughters of these women were screened for the gift. At the age of six years, if they were found to be blessed, they were removed from their home and sent to the palace to begin their training, and then at sixteen they began their official duty as Oracle and Seer. It was important that the Seers remained virgins. This was a promise made to the family – each daughter would be returned unsullied.

Second rule: Sentinels were always the first born sons of a Sentinel, and trained from birth in all aspects of being a great warrior. At the age of thirteen years they were also moved to the palace to learn the special skills they would require. At the age of sixteen they were allowed to return to their homes, have an occupation and marry, until they were called upon to become the protector of a Seer.

Third Rule: Seers and Sentinels were not allowed to marry, nor have any carnal knowledge of each other. This was necessary to keep both lines pure and untainted. If they did marry, none of their children would carry the special gifts.

The function of a Seer was a public role. For the Sentinel it was their sworn duty to be willing to give up their life in the defense of a Seer.

As it is with all things, not everybody was happy with the way things transpired. The mighty God Veros, brother of Eros, was angry because he hadn't been the one chosen to determine the fate of the world.

He was a jealous man, quick to anger, and unrepentant of any action or harm he caused. He was loud, overbearing, and frequently given to long periods of depression. During these times he was morose and sad, and incapable of making any kind of decision.

Eros was the opposite. He was kind, cheerful, and had a loud hearty laugh. He was fair, compassionate, and pleasant to be around. Often he was compared to being like a ray of sunshine on a dark and gloomy day.

After Eros formed the land and the people, he realized that his value as a God was invisible; that in his human form, he was the same as every other person. After much consideration, he appointed the demi-God Altos to take on his human form, to follow his orders and oversee the day to day responsibility for the Seers, Sentinels and the Orbs.

This was one of the most important jobs in the kingdom. Eros chose Altos because he appeared to fulfill all of the requirements needed to mediate between the Gods and the people.

Chapter One

"I'll be damned," Melanie Cain exclaimed. She leaned on the counter of the Petals by Beth Florist Shop where she worked, reading the morning newspaper.

"What's that Mel?" Amy Hutton her boss exclaimed, as she came back into the show room carrying a large bouquet of pink and white carnations in her hands. Placing them on the counter in front of her she asked, "Did something caught your eye this morning?"

"Yes, actually," Melanie replied. "I think my grandmother died. There is an obituary in the paper – right age, right name, and she lived in Farmington too. Doesn't matter though, as far as I am concerned she was a real bitch," she added, her eyes filling with tears.

"Oh Mel, I'm sorry," Amy said coming over, wrapping her arms around her and giving her a big hug. "Were you close?"

"No, as a matter of fact, I haven't seen her since I was a little girl."

Amy gave her a puzzled look, "then what difference does it make that she died?'

Brushing away the tears stinging her eyes Melanie replied, "You are right. Because of her I was raised in a series of foster homes after my parents were killed. The old bag deserted me when she refused to take me in and look after me. Still, she was the only family I had left."

Tearing the page out of the paper, she folded it and put it into her jeans pocket. Carefully she folded the rest of the paper, and put it into the large green garbage can behind the counter.

Amy was surprised. She and Melanie had been best friends and co-workers for a long time, yet this was the first she had spoken about her family. Amy knew that Melanie had a hard upbringing which left her with a tough exterior. She was also a private person who kept everything to herself.

Melanie was unusually quiet the rest of the day. Usually she was happy go lucky, always smiling, always making wise cracks and teasing the customers. Not today though. Today she was quiet and withdrawn- lost in her own thoughts.

As the two girls were ready to leave the shop at the end of the day Melanie said, "I am going to go to Farmington to make sure the old biddy is dead. As far as I know, I am her only living relative – who knows, maybe I'll get lucky, and she left all of her money to me. As her only relative, I should make an appearance." Even though she spoke sarcastically it was a front. She didn't want Amy to see how upset she really was.

"Are you sure that is what you want to do Mel? Wouldn't it be easier to stay here and not put yourself through that? It's not like you are obligated in any way – if she didn't want you, that is."

"I have this Saturday off. If I could have Friday off too I could catch a train to Farmington and be back for work on Monday morning. It's not like I have anything exciting to do this week end any way." she added bitterly, "I am her only living relative, so I guess it is my duty to go whether it's a good idea or not."

"Go ahead and take Friday, I can get one of the part timers to cover for you."

Throughout the years Amy had learned that Melanie worked things out in her own way. She would talk when she was ready, and not before.

Still it bothered Amy to see her friend look so sad and defeated. She shrugged her shoulders, *Melanie can be weird at the best of times, but that's what makes her who she is.*

Chapter Two

Friday morning Melanie caught the six o'clock train to Farmington. That would give her ample time to have something to eat, and find her way to the cemetery. The announcement had read, "Graveside service at two o'clock."

She hoped she didn't have too far to walk. She barely had enough money for her train fare, three cheap meals and a room, if she needed it. She didn't make much working at the florists' shop – enough to pay her rent and utilities, buy groceries and a little for spending. As it was she was using most of her savings to pay for her trip. The train fare had been more expensive than she thought it would be. The bus would have been cheaper, but she wouldn't have arrived in time for the funeral.

During the four hour trip she kept asking herself, *what am I doing. Is going to my grandmother's funeral going to make any difference in how I feel? Yet, as soon as I saw the announcement I had a strong feeling that I have to be there. Maybe I need to do this in order to put this part of my past behind me.*

Throughout her twenty years Melanie had learned to follow her gut feelings, and this time was no different. Although she couldn't understand why, as soon as she had seen the announcement she knew it was important to go to the funeral. It almost felt as though her life and future depended upon her being there.

Stepping off the train onto the station platform, memories of the day she and her mother left came rushing back to her. Some things, such as the train station, the water tower and the entrance to Main Street were the same as they had been fourteen years ago. It felt as though nothing had changed, but in reality everything was different.

Melanie was six when she and her mother had come to visit her grandmother. She remembered hearing the two women arguing before they left to go home, and her mother crying as the train pulled out of the station.. Her grandmother's words still echoed in her head, "for the sake of the child and yours this is how it has to be." The question, "what had to be that way" still haunted her. Melanie never did find out.

She remembered asking her mother why she was crying and her answer, "don't fret yourself child. This has nothing to do with you."

That was the last time she had seen her grandmother. Eighteen months after that visit her parents were killed in a car accident. She kept hoping her grandmother would come and get her, but she never did.

After that, she lived in a series of foster homes. She remembered hearing her social worker tell one of her foster mothers, "The old lady refused to take her and I can't say I blame her. She can be a handful. I hope you have better luck with her than some of the others. That girl is going to end up in trouble, you wait and see."

At sixteen, as soon as she legally able to, Melanie walked away from being a ward of the government. Although she hadn't finished her third form in school, she had been a top student. The fact that she was a quick learner helped her find work at such a young age. Her current job at the flower shop provided an opportunity to become a registered Florist if she decided to follow up and take the course.

After disembarking from the train, Melanie picked up her brightly colored overnight bag. Walking over to the station attendant she asked, "May I leave my bag here for a while?"

"You sure can Miss. Only here for the day?"

"I'm not sure, and this bag is too heavy to pack around with me."

"I'll put it right here behind the counter. We close at nine, so you will need to pick it up before then."

"I am sure my business will be concluded before then. Thank you." Then she began walking toward Main Street. First she had to find a reasonable place to eat lunch, and then find her way to the cemetery.

I should have stayed home, she muttered as she walked past the manicured lawns and flower beds of the station. *I wish to hell I knew what I was doing here.*

Chapter Three

Unsure of where to go, Melanie went inside the Pharmacy and asked the clerk for directions.

"How do I go to get to the cemetery? Is it too far to walk, or do I need to call a taxi?"

"One and a half miles east, down that road. We only have one taxi in town, should I call him for you, may take a while though."

"No thank you, I'm used to walking. I walk twice that far to work every day."

In fact, she was enjoying the walk. The sun was shining, and the air smelled clean, not of heavy exhaust fumes like the city. She was alone on the road, not a vehicle had passed her. She could hear birds singing in the trees, and the breeze whispering in the tree tops. In the city everybody always seemed to be in a hurry, here she noticed how quiet everything was.

The closer she got to the cemetery the more confused she became. Where were the other people who would be attending the funeral? Not one car had passed her the whole time. Had she got the date and time wrong? From the road she glimpsed a long black hearse and one other car in the distance, but the expected crowd of people wasn't there.

Stopping at the cemetery gate, she pulled the newspaper clipping from her pocket and read it again. The date and time were right, but checking her watch she realized she was early. *Maybe people in this area make a point of not showing up until the last minute,* she thought. Certainly this wasn't what she expected. She was hoping to blend into the crowd, and leave as quickly as she could.

Warily she decided to walk toward the hearse and grave site located in the far corner of the grounds. She walked carefully, making sure not to step on any visible graves. She tried to remember the rhyme she had learned as a child about stepping on a grave, but the words wouldn't come to her.

Three men were standing beside an open grave, a plain wooden casket was suspended over a deep gaping hole. From a distance she could see that one of the men was the minister, another obviously a cemetery worker, and the third a very tall good looking man. As she approached the grave site, the tall man left the group and walked towards her.

"May I help you Miss? Are you looking for someone in particular?"

"My name is Melanie Cain and I have come to attend my grandmother's funeral. Mattie Allan was her name. Am I at the right place?"

The man's face turned white. "We weren't expecting any mourners other than family, and we weren't sure if there was any family left to show up. I understand the family was estranged."

"Just me," Melanie replied flippantly, "and I haven't seen her since I was six years old. I'm her granddaughter and the only one left, so I guess you could say all of her family is here."

The young man looked her up and down. "I see. If you can prove that you are who you say you are, that changes everything, and not necessarily for good." Under his breath he added. "I knew this was too easy."

"Come, he said "we might as well get started."

The other men looked at him and he gave them a nod. Melanie was ushered to the side of the casket; the minister stepped to the head and said a few brief words. In less than five minutes the ceremony was over.

Melanie turned to walk away hiding the tears in her eyes. *Now I am truly alone in this world. Before I knew at least I had a grandmother, even though we weren't in contact with each other, now there is no one I can call my own.*

The young man walked over to her and said "I am Adam Brighton, your grandmother's attorney, may I drive you back to town? There are some things we need to discuss. We can go directly to my office and take care of our business right away."

Melanie thought to herself, *He sounds like a pompous ass. What a shame someone so young and good looking sounds like that.*

"Thank you for your offer, but I prefer to walk back," she responded. *Be damned if I'm going to listen to him all the way back to town.*

"Please Miss Cain, we really do need to talk. Could you arrange then to meet me at my office at four o'clock?" he said handing her his business card. "My office is located beside the mercantile store."

"I guess so" she answered. *I guess I need to hear what he has to say and find a place to stay tonight. I might as well get all of the necessities done while I am here because I have no intention of ever coming back again.*

"Yes, I will be at your office by four." She replied, turning her back and walking away from him. In the background she heard the clods of dirt landing on top of the casket.

This was more difficult than I expected it to be. Walking back will give me time to compose my thoughts and prepare myself for what is to come. I'll bet the old lady has a pile of debts that I am going to have to pay off. That would just be my luck.

Chapter Four

Melanie walked slowly back to town. The sun had disappeared behind a cloud, and a cool breeze caused the leaves to flutter. She shivered as the breeze whipped around her.

Who is lawyer Adam Brighton and what was he to my grandmother? Why is he so anxious to see me? If he is grandma's attorney, then he must know the whole story about why I am alone.

A fresh tear trickled down her cheek. Then taking a deep breath, she resolved *I will see what he has to say, and if there is a late train, I will go home tonight.*

She went directly to the station where she retrieved her overnight bag from safe keeping. She also checked the train schedule, which was predominantly posted on the wall, but the next train didn't leave until the afternoon of the next day.

Disappointed, she took her case into the bathroom, tidied up her hair, washed the dust from the road and the tear streaks off her face. Noting she had time to spare, she went into the station coffee shop and ordered a cup of tea and a cookie. She was worried about spending too much of her money until she knew what one nights lodging was going to cost. Even though she was being extremely careful, her limited funds were rapidly disappearing.

At exactly four o'clock she entered the reception area of Lawyer Brighton's office. An older woman in a navy blue pant suit sat at the desk. Before Melanie had a chance to say anything the woman looked up at her and asked, "Are you Melanie Caine?"

"Yes," she replied.

"Come right in, Lawyer Brighton is expecting you. You can leave your overnight bag here if you wish. I'll make sure nothing happens to it."

She led Melanie down a short hallway to a large bright office. She was surprised. Lawyer Brighton seemed so stodgy when he spoke to her, and this modern office wasn't what she expected. She had assumed it would be dark and cramped, just like his personality.

In front of a window was a large mahogany desk with a lap top sitting on it. A well-used high backed swivel chair sat behind the desk. In one corner sat a black leather chair and sofa grouping around a glass coffee table. The beige walls were decorated with diplomas and colorful paintings.

"Can I get you something to drink while you are waiting?" The receptionist asked.

"No thank you, I had a cup of tea at the station before I came."

Adam Brighton came through the door making his way to the desk. "Please sit Miss Cain," he said, indicating a chair in front of the desk. Melanie sat as she was directed, her knees together, her hands folded primly in her lap.

"Do you have any identification?" He asked abruptly.

Digging into her purse she pulled out her wallet and found the plasticized copy of her birth certificate and her social insurance card. She handed them to him without saying a word.

He perused them carefully, and then double checked her birth date and deceased parents' names. "Can't be too careful these days," he said.

He opened the top right drawer of his desk and pulled out an official looking brown envelope. Opening the envelope he took out a sheaf of papers and laid them on the desk in front of him. Then he put the envelope back into the drawer.

Melanie wanted to scream at him, *you are wasting my time and yours, so stop being so persnickety and get on with it.*

Finally he looked up at her, "As Mattie's only living relative she has bequeathed you her small financial estate, and her home located on three prime acres of land. The town has been attempting to purchase this land for some time, so you have the option of selling it to them. I can make all of the arrangements for you if you wish."

Melanie looked at him, shock of his revelation registered on her face. "Are you sure? She refused to acknowledge me when she was alive, why would she do this when she is dead?" Then in the next breath she asked, "Do I even get to see the house and land before I decide to sell them?"

"Of course," he replied. When he had taken the papers out of the envelope he had also removed a set of keys. "These are the keys to the house. This larger one is for the front door and the other three are for the rooms she kept locked upstairs. She lived on the main floor. I'll be glad to take you there if you wish, as soon as we are done here."

"I would like that," Melanie replied feeling completely overwhelmed. Within minutes Lawyer Brighton put on his jacket, and told the receptionist where they were going. He picked up her overnight bag and escorted her to his car.

Once again she was surprised when she saw his car. It was a two seater red convertible. For some reason she had in her mind something entirely different. They were silent as he drove along the road.

Adam Brighton was fretting. *I'll be glad when this over. I hope she doesn't begin asking a bunch of questions, just decides to sell the house and land and be on her way. I can't help but wonder if she even knows of the distinct talents her grandmother possessed. I wish she would have stayed away and then this whole business would have come to an end. If she searches hard enough and finds the orbs, then whatever Mattie tried so desperately to protect her from will happen.*

On the drive Melanie thought, *everything is happening too fast. I have gone from florist apprentice to heiress in one day. All of this seems too good to be true. Previous experiences have taught me that when things seem this way, they usually are. I wonder what the catch is.*

Chapter Five

Adam Brighton drove two miles north of town and then turned into a tree lined driveway. The tall cylindrical shaped trees rose like sentinels on both sides of the road. At the end of the driveway stood an old, two story, manor house that must have been over one hundred years old. Lush green lawns, interspersed with flower beds of bright colors, surrounded the house

When lawyer Brighton helped her out of the car Melanie turned to him and exclaimed, "It's just as I remember, nothing has changed."

Taking her overnight bag from behind the seat he replied, "Mattie had the inside brought up to code and modernized several years ago. She had plumbers, electricians and roofers here for weeks. She thought that if she ever had to sell, she would get a better price. She was like that, always thinking, and always one step ahead of everyone else."

Walking up to the front door he said, "she lived on the ground floor. She wasn't able to climb the stairs anymore so she closed off the upstairs rooms and locked them. As far as I know nobody has been up there for ages. Her knees were bad, and it was costing her a fortune to heat the whole house."

"What did she die from? You haven't mentioned anything yet."

"I think she just got tired. She hadn't been in the best of health for a long time and was adamant about not moving into town to the seniors lodge, said she would die before she did that. I tried several times to get her to reconsider, but that was like talking to a brick wall. She was a stubborn old girl. Once Mattie made up her mind about something she wouldn't change it."

Unlocking the front door, he handed her the key ring and escorted her into a hallway. Melanie inhaled deeply, expecting the smell of musk, mold and decay. Instead it was the familiar scent of her grandmother's perfume, White Gardenia.

Leading her down the hallway past two closed door he added, "Mattie used the parlor as a sitting room. There is a kitchen, a smaller parlor which she used as a bedroom, and she put in a modern bathroom several years ago. She was quite content living here.

Mattie always had lots of company, and when my dad was alive he used to check on her every day. She always referred to him as "my best friend." They had a unique special arrangement between them. After dad passed I tried to come out here as often as I could. Mattie and my grandfather were old friends, and when he passed away, my dad looked after her.

"I have one question. If she had so many so called friends, why were none of them at the cemetery today?"

"That's the way she wanted it. No mourning, no tears, simply remembering the happy times they had together."

"Did she ever say anything about me?" Melanie asked. He either didn't hear her question, or ignored it.

"Well," he said, "this is all yours now. Let's see if there is any food here. If not we can go back to town, pick up a few things, and come back tomorrow. Where are you staying? I can drop you off there."

"I think I'll stay here tonight," Melanie replied. She felt too embarrassed to tell him that she couldn't afford to stay anywhere. "Let's take a look and see if there is anything I can use."

Opening and closing the cupboard doors she found tea, a couple of tins of biscuits and several cans of mushroom soup. "I don't think I will starve in one night. This is more than enough."

"Okay if that's what you want to do," Lawyer Brighton commented. "I'll come by first thing in the morning. By the way you can call me Adam. If I'm to be your lawyer, we don't need to be so formal. May I call you Melanie?"

"Yes, I would like that. When somebody calls me Miss Cain I'm not sure if it's me they are talking to."

Taking a card out of his pocket he wrote a number on it and handed it to her. "This is my personal cell number. Call me if you change your mind or need anything, and make sure you lock the doors behind me. Even though not much happens around here, it's better to be cautious."

Melanie walked to the door with him and watched him walk down the steps. When the door closed, he heard the click of the lock.

Once in his car he sat staring at the house for a long time. *Oh Mattie, what is going to happen now? She has no idea what she has walked into. I wish she had stayed away. I have a feeling that she is just as stubborn as you were. It must run in the family.*

Maybe she won't find the orbs and all of my worrying will be for nothing. After she leaves I will search until I find them myself, and then lock them away so that nobody ever finds them again.

As he drove away he knew the orbs weren't of any value to just anybody. Their only value was to a Seer. He had felt the call of the Sentinel as she walked toward her grandmother's grave. Melanie Cain was now his responsibility – like it or not.

Chapter Six

Melanie left her overnight bag in the hallway by the door and walked back to the kitchen. She was hungry. She found a kettle, rinsed it well, filled it half-full of water and then put it on the stove to boil. She opened a can of soup and emptied it into a saucepan. When the water had boiled, she made a mug of Earl Grey tea. She opened a tin of biscuits and ate several with her soup.

When finished eating she put the dishes into the sink, refilled her tea cup and thought, *girl, it's time to find out what you got.*

The bathroom was simple, but functional. – a shower in one corner, a toilet, and vanity with a single white sink. Pink towels and face cloths hung on the towel racks.

The bedroom, which was larger than she thought, was a surprise. The walls were painted a soft yellow, with a floral bed-cover and matching drapes. There was a small closet and a large dresser. A colorful painting signed by her grandmother hung on the wall. The closet was empty as were the drawers, but some of her grandmothers personal items still remained on top of the dresser.

From there she walked to the parlor. Right away Melanie knew this was going to be her favorite room. Two comfortable, dark blue, sofas sat at a ninety degree angle to each other and a coffee table was centered in front of them. A multi-colored, blue braided scatter rug was under the coffee table.

On another wall was a grouping of pale green chairs in front of a stone fire place. Floor to ceiling book shelves, crammed with books, filled the spaces on both sides of the fireplace. A basket with a half knitted mitt rested beside one of the chairs. A small television set was within eye view of the chairs and the sofas. Melanie sensed this was the room her grandmother used most of the time.

Various pieces of antique furniture covered with nick knacks were scattered around the room. More paintings decorated the walls. At first glance it appeared crowded, but the room had a cozy feel. Knitted Afghans lay on the back of the sofas and one chair.

She sat down on one of the sofas, leaned back, and continued to sip her tea. She wished she had known her grandmother better. She loved this room, and, even though many years had passed, she felt her grandmother's presence embracing her.

After a while she got up and went into the remaining rooms. Two of them contained furniture covered with white sheets making their purpose unknown. Heavy brocaded drapes covered the windows.

She shivered, and pulled the doors closed, resolving to come back in the daylight. *It will be interesting to see what is hidden under those dust covers, but first I want to see what is upstairs.*

She took the key ring with her because Lawyer Brighton had mentioned her grandmother kept the rooms upstairs closed, and locked.

The first room she went into was a bedroom. A quilted mattress cover protected the bed. There were no pictures on the wall, nor any signs that anyone had been in there for a long time. The room was simply furnished with a bed, a tall dresser, and a plain wooden chair. Old fashioned green blinds covered the window.

I wonder if this used to be my mother's room when she was a child she mused. Even knowing there was nothing in the room; she opened and closed all of the drawers. They were empty as expected.

She opened the closed doors of the closet, which was also empty, and ran her finger tips along the top shelf. They brushed against something hard. Pulling the chair closer, she climbed on top of it and reached for whatever her hand had touched.

She was disappointed to see it was a dusty, dirty, glass ball. Looking around, not seeing anything she could use to wipe the dirt off, she went back downstairs to the kitchen, found a soft cloth and dampened it.

Back upstairs she began scrubbing at the dirt. The ball began to feel warm in her hand. *It's your over active imagination girl* she thought as she scrubbed at one spot that refused to come clean. As she wiped the last of the spots off the glass ball, it began to glow. As she watched, the glow became stronger.

What the hell.... Holding the ball in her hand she sat down on the wooden chair and began to study it. On a closer look, the object in her hand reminded her of one of those glass balls that a fortune teller peers into before they tell you your fortune. *I wonder what is making it do this.* Immediately her mind went to the comic book character Superman and his kryptonite. She giggled out loud.

Inside the orb she began seeing images of buildings, and people, and after some time, she became aware that a story was taking place inside the glass ball.

Melanie began to feel strange, and suddenly she was inside the glass ball, observing what was happening. She could hear the grunts of the two men fighting, and smell the dust being raised by their feet.

As the picture moved in front of Melanie, two people, one of them thousands of miles away felt a jolt of electricity. Adam Brighton cursed. He knew immediately Melanie had found one of the glass orbs.

Across the ocean in the African town of Zahara a man, a General in the Army, was awakened from a dream. He didn't know what the dream meant, but he sensed it was important, and involved a glass ball. Immediately the memory of an ancient tale told by his father came to his mind. He was a superstitious man who believed dreams carried message. He decided first thing in the morning he would find someone who was capable of interpreting his dream.

Fascinated Melanie watched the story unfold in front of her. Instinctively, she knew the background of what and why this altercation was taking place.

* * *

Up until this point, Veros had been quietly fuming about his perceived unfairness of all that had transpired. As a result he became bitter and angry with those around him. When he learned that once again he had been overlooked, and Altos had been appointed to the earthly liaison position, he was furious.

He waited for Altos in an alley and, when he saw him approaching, attacked him. They fought furiously, the sound of their mighty swords echoing throughout the town. The sky turned black, lightening snaked its way to the ground, and thunder rolled in the heavens. The people of the town became afraid as they witnessed the power of the angry Gods.

A runner came to Eros' room where he was resting after his noon meal. "You must come quickly Eros," he said breathlessly. "Veros and Altos are waging a mighty battle. Their fighting has upset the heavens, and people are cowering in their homes, afraid of what may come.

Calling to the captain of his personal guard to bring men and follow him, Eros left with the runner to stop the fighting. When he arrived he saw Altos had slain Veros, and cut off his head.

Pain seared through him. This isn't what he had intended. He knelt beside the body of his brother and wept.

"What happened here?" he demanded of Altos.

"I was walking past the alley and he attacked me," he replied, "I had no choice but to defend myself."

"Did you have to kill him, and then remove his head like a common criminal?"

"He left me no choice, it was him or me. Would you have preferred for your brother to have killed me, and I was the one lying there ?"

Eros didn't answer him. He turned and addressed one of the guards, "go to the palace and return with a cart for my brother's body" He sat on the ground, cradling the head of his brother in his lap until the cart arrived, then moved his brother's body to the palace.

The mourning period for a God was thirty days. The body of the God Veros was placed in a gold coffin and lay in state for the people to come and grieve. On the morning of the thirtieth day the coffin was loaded upon a horse driven cart covered in black cloth. Eros and a contingent of his personal guards took the body of Veros to lie in a sacred place hidden in the hills. Watchmen observed their passage stopping anyone from the city who tried to follow.

During his time of grieving, Eros instructed his spies keep a close secret watch over Altos. Too late he realized he had made a mistake, and he was very angry. From the day his brother was killed, Eros considered Altos a spawn of the black God, and from then on he and his descendants would be punished by striving to gain control of the world and failing.

Eros continued to grieve in silence, always watching, always listening to see what Altos would do next. The more he watched the more he realized that choosing Altos over his brother Veros had put the entire world in danger. Giving Altos power over the orbs and the responsibility of overlooking the Delphi Temple and the Oracles made him a dangerous man.

Soon he began hearing rumors that Altos was demanding larger and larger payments to visit the Oracle. Those who could pay gained admittance, but others were denied unless they too could produce gold. The poor and needy no longer had access.

Eros began keeping a careful accounting of the number of people who visited the oracle and the amount of money that was being turned into the temple treasurer. Soon, it became evident that less and less gold was reaching the coffers to support the Temple, and that Altos was becoming a rich man. More than once he was heard boasting as he sat in the taverns buying drinks, that soon he would be ruling the world, and be greater than the God Eros. The time and place were of his choosing – the mystery of the orbs was his secret until then.

He gathered a group of unsavory men around himself and paid for small favors, using the gold he stole from the oracle – kill this man, rape that one's wife and daughters. Soon the people in the town feared him. He forced the politicians and merchants to pay for his protection. If they refused, he sent his band of cut throats to change their minds. Eros appointed twenty-four hour protection for the Seers. These young nubile girls were sacred and were promised to be returned to their parents untouched by any man. Eros knew that the sweet fumes emanating from the earth left the Sears incapacitated at the end of each day – open and vulnerable to anyone who wished to prey upon them.

His concern grew as he continued to hear stories that Altos and his band of thugs had been intercepted approaching the Seer's living quarters. One had been driven off and killed by one of the guards, but, not without first revealing what Altos had in mind.

Eros became angrier. He had trusted Altos with the most precious commodities of his kingdom, and to hear rumors of the possible rape and kidnapping of the Oracles distressed him greatly. One day he called the Captain of the Guard to his room.

"Clavius, I want you to take two of your best men, have them do favors for Altos and gain his trust. I have to know for sure what he is up to, and the only way to accomplish this is to have men close by him."

That very night the two young guards began following Altos' men around the town. Dressed as rich merchants they began buying drinks and gambling with them. Naturally they lost a great deal of money. The thugs eagerly became accustomed to their presence. The more drink they bought, the more money they lost, the freer the men's tongues became

After several weeks, Marco, the youngest of the guards, reported to Clavius, "one the guards protecting the Sears has been compromised. Altos has been playing his men one against the other, promising them the body of a virgin Seer to warm their beds. He himself is making plans to deflower each one of them. I am afraid for their safety."

As soon as Clavius reported this information to Eros, all of the current guards were replaced and sent to a training camp far away from the city. Even this didn't comfort him, nor ensure the safety of the Seers. With the offer of enough money, and the dangling of a virgin Seer as a reward, what happened once could easily happen again

Eros developed a plan. The people believed the Seers and listened to whatever they were told. Altos was becoming more and more dangerous. Eros planned to remove the orbs and replace them with fakes, but when he went to do this, he discovered he was too late. Somebody had already replaced the originals with fakes. Altos had stolen and hidden the real ones, and nobody knew where they were.

Fully realizing the danger to his world Eros enlisted the help of Henna, the Goddess of Women's Virtue, to help him. He announced during his next daily council meeting that a new talented and gifted Seer from a distant land was coming to the Temple. Not only was she very beautiful, but she had the ability to see more, with greater accuracy.

Altos was intrigued. He was the first to seek out her wisdom, and was immediately captivated by her beauty and smile. Each day he went to her, and slowly she enticed him into her web. One morning, when he was waiting for her in the hallway, she put out her hand and touched his arm. The next morning, when she saw him standing in the same place, she gave him a smile that lit up her whole face. Quickly he became infatuated with her.

One morning, seeing she was alone, he spoke to her, "I must be with you. May I come to your room after dark?"

At first she refused his advances, but after several such attempts she replied "meet me tonight in the Moon garden at midnight."

Altos was beside himself with excitement and pleased to find her waiting when he arrived. She wore a silver dress which shimmered in the moonlight, her long loose, white hair flowing down her back to her waist.

They spoke only a few words, and when she left, she kissed his cheeks on either side of his lips. Night after night they met in the secret Garden and, each time he left, his body ached with lust. They continued to meet until the night he reached out for her as she was preparing to leave. He pulled her into his arms, and began kissing her.

Taking her hand he placed it on his erection, "see how desperately I want you. What can I give you so that you will consent to come to my bed?"

At first Henna didn't reply, and then she answered, "I wish to hold and see the orbs all in one place. Allow me this favor, and I will give you that night in your bed you so desire."

"What makes you think I have them?" Altos asked, "They are in the Temple, the Seers use them every day."

Henna didn't answer him. Instead, she took one of his hands and placed it on her breast, with her other, she gripped his manhood. "We both know the ones in use are fakes. I want to see the real ones."

At first Altos was taken back that she knew fakes were being used, but his lust filled brain didn't stop to question how she knew. He was beside himself with happiness. If that was all it was going to take to get her into his bed, he would gladly accommodate her. "Come to my bed chamber tomorrow night and I will have them for you."

"I will also have something special for you," she replied, smiling at him, her eyes filled with promise.

He was waiting for her when she slipped into his room. "This is forbidden," she said. "I am late because I had to be sure I wasn't seen coming in here." She walked over and kissed him on the lips and asked breathlessly, "did you bring the orbs with you? I can hardly wait to see them."

"Yes, I have them. Wait here." He went into his closet, and from the back brought out a jeweled encrusted case.

She gasped when she saw the orbs lying inside the box. "They are so beautiful, may I touch them? I have never seen anything so beautiful."

One at a time Henna took the orbs out of the box and held them in her lap. Without Altos being aware of what she was doing, she examined each of them to be sure it was real

Altos watched her, but after several minutes he said, "That's enough". Taking the orbs from her hands, he put them back into the case, and placed it on a nearby table.

"Now, he said to her in his steely voice, "now it is your turn to please me," and he grabbed at her.

Henna was well prepared for what she knew was coming next. "Don't be in such a hurry we have all night," she said, smiling at him

Walking over to the table, she poured two glasses of wine. Leaving hers on the table she handed a glass to Altos. Before he could say anything, she reached down and pulled her dress over her head, standing before him in all her naked glory – her long white hair covering her breasts.

Altos downed his glass of wine and reached for her, but she danced away, taking his wineglass with her. She filled it again and handed it back to him. Then she walked over to the chaise lounge, located under the window, laid down and posed provocatively.

She whispered, "Come and join me. I am ready."

Altos tossed back the glass of wine, quickly removed his shirt and trousers, and fell on top of her. Pawing at her with his hands, he pushed her thighs apart eager to be inside her. Before he could begin she heard a sigh, and his heavy body collapsed on top of her.

Henna breathed a sigh of relief. The sleeping potion she had put in the wine before sending it to his room had rendered him unconscious. She smiled. The amount of wine he drank would keep him asleep until the next afternoon.

When she was sure he wouldn't wake up she pushed his limp body off her. Just letting him touch her made her feel dirty. Quickly she put on her dress, picked up the case with the orbs and slipped out the door. Marco, her newly appointed guardian was waiting for her.

"Are you alright my lady? Did he hurt you?"

"No, I am fine, but he is a pig," she shuddered. "I can barely wait to have a bath and wash the feel of his hands off me."

The next afternoon, when Altos awoke, he felt groggy and disorientated. At first he had difficulty remembering where he was, and what had taken place the evening before, but as his memory returned, he realized Henna had played him for a fool.

He staggered to his feet first checking the table to see if the case with the orbs was still there. When there was no evidence of it he frantically dug through his closet, but they were gone.

"She is not going to get away with his," he screamed into the empty room. "They are mine and I intend to get them back and be the ruler of the world. Once I have the orbs in my hands, I will take her first, and then give her to my men. If she doesn't confess and tell me who put her up to this trick, she definitely will after they are done with her. I have to know. If she survives, I will parade her broken naked body through the streets. No one will ever again believe anything she has to say."

Altos knew that Henna would be heavily guarded, and he wouldn't be able to get past them that night. After much thinking he developed a plan. He would wait for her in his usual place in the hallway, grab her and bring her back to his room. He would station men along the way with strict orders to kill any guard who tried to follow him.

The next morning Henna walked down the hall knowing Altos would approach her. Guards were stationed at both ends, and at the side entrances, in case he appeared. Eros had begged her to leave the night before, but she refused.

"I am not in the habit of running from danger," she had told him, and wasn't surprised when a hand grabbed her arm and pulled her into the shadows.

"Where are they," Altos hissed in her face.

"Where are what?" She replied calmly, although she didn't feel that way. She tried to pull her arm away, but he held on tighter.

"Don't you dare play stupid with me," he said, striking her across the face. "The orbs – where are they?"

Glaring back at him she replied, "Safe, some place where you can't get them. Now take your filthy hands off me."

"Tell me," he said, drawing back his fist and punching her in the stomach. Henna doubled over. *No person had ever dared lay a hand on me this way. Doesn't he realize I am a Goddess?*

He yanked on her hair, pulling her upright, "You either tell me where they are now, or I will give you to my men to do with as they wish. Once they are finished, you will wish you had spoken up before."

He began dragging her down an adjoining hallway. She struck out at him connecting with his nose. He let out a growl and put his hand to his face. Blood was running between his fingers.

She stared at him, her eyes glowing as red as fire. "I curse you, and I curse our sons, and their sons, and their son's sons. Until the end of time they will seek to own the orbs and the power that goes with them, but will never succeed. They will never have what they desire most."

Altos launched himself at her, knocking her to the ground, one hand tugging at the hem of her dress. "I am not going to wait to get you to my room; I will show you right here and now what I am capable of. Scream all you want, no one is going to hear you."

He slapped her across the face again. "You will beg to tell me what I want to know before I am finished with you."

Suddenly he crumpled on top her, deathly still. She lay under him struggling to catch her breath; her face stinging from the blows Altos had dealt her.

"Are you all right my lady?" Marco asked, "I got here as fast as I could."

"Yes, just get him off me. I can't breathe."

Marco was a big strong man. With little effort he picked Altos up and threw him against the wall. "Come we must get out of here before he wakes up, or one of his men come looking for him."

He helped Henna to her feet. When he saw her bruised face he turned white. "You are bleeding; we must get you some help."

"Do not worry, it is nothing. There is no time for that. I must get to the orbs and hide them where Altos will never find them, and then I must hide. Altos will kill me if he gets his hands on me again."

Marco put his arm around Henna's waist and led her out of the hallway into the temple. "Leave them," he told her," he will not find them today. I must get you away now; we will come back after dark to retrieve them."

"No, I must leave as quickly as I can. I can't stay here."

She led him to the seat of the Oracle. As he watched she stepped over the wall and reached into a small niche in the wall above where the fumes emanated. She pulled out the jeweled encrusted case, and then taking Marco by the hand led him to a hidden door, and through a labyrinth of tunnels until they stood at the mouth of a cave.

"Where are we?" he asked

"In the hills above the city," she replied. "This is an escape route for the Oracles in case the city was overrun by a foreign army."

From on high, Eros watched as the events unfolded beneath him. In the quiet of the cave he spoke to them, "Henna leave here and return to your normal way of life. Your duty is done, you have saved the orbs. Marco, you have also served me well, go with her and protect her. From now on the Seer shall be the only one who can use the power of the orbs. You are now Henna's Sentinel, and your duty is to protect her and the orbs. This too will pass from generation to generation along your family line – one Seer – one Sentinel."

To Henna he said, "find a safe place for the orbs inside this cave, and then run from here as fast as you can."

Turning, Henna walked toward the back of the cave and entered another tunnel. After walking a short distance she spotted a deep alcove in the wall. Reverently she placed the case containing the orbs into the alcove pushing them as far back as she could reach.

She retraced her steps to the mouth of the cave, and taking Marco's hand they quickly made their way down the barely visible foot path which led to the cave entrance.

Suddenly there was a deep rumble in the earth. The the hill began to shake and a huge cloud of dust rushed from the mouth of the cave. When the dust settled, the cave entrance had disappeared. Together they made their way out of the city and disappeared

* * *

The orb turned dark. When Melanie came to, she was lying on the floor, the chair was overturned, and the glass orb was tightly clutched in her hand. The first time she tried to sit up she felt nauseated and dizzy, but after several attempts, managed to stagger from the bedroom, down the stairs, and into the parlor.

Placing the orb on the coffee table in front of her, she pulled the Afghan off the back of the sofa, lay down and covered herself. Even the weight of the heavy blanket wasn't enough to stop her shivering.

Chapter Seven

Suddenly General Alexander Fatima woke to a jolt, like electrify and a thundering sound. The sound, like the bass of a boom box but far away, began in the back of his head and moved to the front. It was loud enough to be irritating, but not close enough to identify where it was coming from. Something primal was happening, and on some deeper level he knew that it was important.

The young, dark haired, naked woman beside him stirred. "After last night how can you be awake already?" she purred like a satisfied kitten. She ran her hand over his chest and then down toward his thigh.

"Don't," he said sharply.

"Why not, it looks to me that you are more than ready to take up where we left off."

"Don't touch me," he replied edgily, lifting her hand and moving it away. When she touched him again he became angry, "get out now."

"Baby, what did I do wrong?"

Through gritted teeth he shouted at her. "Didn't you hear me? I said get out. Now!"

He reached over to his bedside table, and pushed a button on the intercom. Immediately a very large dark man opened the bedroom door and walked in.

"Get her out of here. Pay her off and get rid of her."

The girl looked first at Alex, and then at the man in the doorway. Nonchalantly she got out of the bed and walked naked to the bathroom, picking up her scattered clothing along the way.

Alexander lay back on his bed, his head pounding from the loud incessant noise in his ears. He closed his eyes. He heard the man and woman talking, the door opened, and then she was gone

"What's going on Alex?" Hamad DeManuel asked.

"Can you hear that sound? It's like the beating of a drum, and its driving me crazy. Go find out where it is coming from and make it stop."

"I don't hear anything. Shall I call the Doctor?" He came to the side of the bed and rearranged Alex's pillow. "Put your head back and rest, I will get one of your headache tablets."

Alex groaned, "Please do." Putting his hands to his ears, he said, "And do something to make that noise stop. Bring me a drink."

Hamad left, and quickly returned. He handed Alex a glass with two ounces of scotch and a morphine-based tablet. "One of these days mixing the two is going to kill you."

Alex put the tablet into his mouth and emptied the glass of scotch, "go away now. Let me rest, but before you go, make sure Lila is gone, and don't bring her to me again. In fact, she can become one of your personal play things. I don't want her asking any questions."

"Yes Sir," Hamad said as he left the room, closing the door behind him. He never minded accepting Alex's left overs. In fact, he was already looking forward to spending some private time with this one.

Alex fell asleep, and as usual the dream returned. Always it was the same – four gold balls spinning just out of reach of his fingertips. An old man dressed in a white robe was always sitting in the same corner. Usually he ignored Alex's attempts to capture the balls,

Today the dream was different. The old man said, "The orbs are in play. Gather the Seer and all four orbs, and you will rule the world."

Several hours later when Alex awoke, his headache was gone. He knew the ancient story of the orbs because it had been passed down through history by the men in his family. Part of the destiny of his family was to gather the orbs into their hands. When they had all of them, they were destined to become the most powerful rulers the world has ever known.

Alec felt exhilarated. *Now the world is going to become mine and I will be unstoppable.*

Alexander Fatima was the only son of a tribal king who had married an English woman. He had gone to the best English schools and then, at an early age, became a military leader in his own right.

While he was away at school his uncle led a coup against the leaders of the country. He was a ruthless man, and by the time he became king, Alex's mother and father were both dead.

Alexander quit school, came home, and began the fight to regain the kingship that should have been his by right of birth. It had been a long bloody war, but eventually his rebel army had defeated the leaders and taken back his legacy. He changed from the happy go lucky rich boy to a man bent upon revenge. He ruled his country with the iron hand of a dictator.

The dream of the orbs greatly disturbed him. *What does it mean?*

Hamad was not only his personal body guard but his only friend, the one man he dared to trust. As he often did, he invited Hamad to join him for a drink before supper.

"You are not yourself these days," Hamad remarked as he stood at the bar mixing their drinks. He picked up the glasss, and walked over to Alex, handing him one. "What's going on?"

Alex ignored his question. "What did you do with the girl?"

"I used her a several times and then let her go. It will be some time before she wants another man."

"I hope you didn't hurt her too badly. We don't need talk around the city about our sexual proclivities here at the palace."

"I assure you she walked out of here on her own."

Alex smiled knowingly. Hamad had an unusual sexual appetite.

"Trust me Alex; she won't want anybody to know what went on here. Now, what is going on with you?"

Alex stared at the drink in his hand for a long time and then told Hamad about his dream. Both had been raised to be great believers in dreams.

"What do you think it means?" Hamad asked.

"That's the thing, I don't know. All I know is that it's important that I find out."

"I have an idea," Hamad replied. "There is one way to find out. You must go to the temple of El-Shada and speak with the Ancient One. It is said he is a dream reader. He may know what this means."

Alex thought for a brief moment. "As usual you are right, we will leave first thing in the morning."

"Shall I arrange some entertainment for you tonight?"

"No, I think not if we are going to leave early in the morning, although it sounds like a good idea."

Early the next morning, before the sun was up, Alec and Hamad began the two hour drive through the desert to the temple at El-Shada. When they arrived, they were immediately ushered into the presence of the Ancient One.

He was a tiny, wizened, old man dressed in a white robe that appeared far too big on him. He sat in a large armchair which made him look like a child. Hamad and Alex both fell to their knees and bowed their heads to the floor, a tribute of honor for being allowed in his presence.

"Would you care to have something to eat or drink? You must have been up and on the road early this morning."

Alex and Hamad then stood up and looked at each other. Alex said, "We are fine thank you."

"I knew you would be coming and why," the Ancient One said. "But first must you tell me what you want from me."

"Nearly every night since I was a boy I have had the same dream. There are four orbs spinning just beyond my reach and I can't catch them. Then the dream changed. The old man in the dream told me "the orbs are in play once again – now is the time to go and find them. When I possess them, and the Seer who guards them, I will rule the world."

The ancient one smiled, "at last, it has been many years. I thought the orbs had been lost." Then he told them the ancient story of the Seer and the orbs.

"Sit down and do not move," the ancient one said, indicating two chairs in front of him. Then he focused his eyes on something over Alex's right shoulder. Alex and Hamad sat there not moving or speaking.

After about fifteen minutes the Ancient One blinked and turned to Alex. "The orbs are in play but only one so far. You .must wait until all are in one place."

Alex answered impatiently, "I will send one of my men to retrieve it, Where is it?"

The ancient one put his hand up as if to stop him, "I do not know yet. You have to wait." Then he waved his hand dismissing them. "I will send word to you as soon as I know, but until then you must exercise patience."

Alex and Hamad left. On the drive home Alex asked, "Do you believe what he said?"

Hamad thought for several seconds and replied, "I'm not sure. I guess we will have to wait and see what this leads to."

"As usual, you are right Hamad. We will celebrate together tonight. Phone ahead and arrange for some entertainment – fresh young women, eager to please. It has been two days since I have had a woman"

Hamad smiled, "I am glad to hear things are getting back to normal. You have been much too distracted these last few days. You were beginning to worry me."

He picked up his cell phone, dialed and spoke to somebody on the other end. "All is arranged Alex."

"Perhaps you wish to join me? It's always more interesting that way."

Hamad smiled. "I will be glad to."

Chapter Eight

Knowing Melanie had found one of the orbs kept Adam Brighton awake and pacing his living room for the rest of the night. First of all, he was angry at her. *Why did she have to come here for the funeral? Why didn't she simply stay away? I have a life of my own, or rather did have. I have a girlfriend and a profession I love. Why do I have to give up my life for Melanie Cain? Why didn't my father keep his damn secrets to himself? Why do I have to be part of this? I don't even like her. She is just a smart mouthed kid that I am now obligated to be around whether I want to be or not.*

Even though he paced and railed against the injustice of how he had born and what he had been born to do, he knew that he had little choice. His father had told him of his obligation when he was barely old enough to understand. The only questions left unanswered were when and who.

He showered, and dressed in a pair of well-fitting blue jeans and a blue denim shirt. Since it was Saturday he didn't need to wear his usual suit and tie. It was bad enough to have to wear one all week, he liked to be casual on the weekends. By the time he was ready, the grocery store was open. He stopped, picked up a few items, and drove out of town.

When he arrived at Melanie's, the house was dark except for a dim light coming from the parlor. He knocked on the door, but there was no answer. He knocked again and still nothing.

Yesterday, after returning to his office, he had found another set of keys in his desk drawer. A tag, written in his father's precise hand, read Mattie's keys.

He let himself into the house using one of the keys to unlock the door. "Melanie," he called out, but there was no answer. He headed straight for the parlor, fighting back a gut feeling that something was very wrong.

When he walked through the door he saw Melanie asleep on the sofa sporting a large purple bruise on her forehead. *That wasn't there when I left yesterday.* He looked for the rise and fall of her chest to see if she was breathing.

Assuring himself that she was alive he went into the kitchen. After much searching he found a coffee maker and a container of coffee. Making as much noise as possible, he put the groceries away, hoping the noise would wake her up.

When the coffee was ready, he filled two large mugs and went back to the parlor. "Wake up sleepy head," he announced loudly.

Melanie opened her eyes and looked around. When she saw him, she sat up straight, "How did you get in here? I know I locked the door after you left."

"Good morning to you too. I found an extra set of keys in my desk drawer. When you didn't answer the door, I let myself in. "Here" he said, handing one of the cups of coffee. "This will help wake you up. Hope you don't need milk or sugar, because I forgot to buy them this morning."

Accepting the cup from his hand Melanie replied, "I usually drink mine black anyway."

He sat down on the opposite sofa. They sat in silence, each aware of the presence of the other. He watched as Melanie sipped her hot coffee. When she appeared more relaxed he asked, "how did you get that bruise on your forehead?"

"I fell off a chair," she replied.

He waited for her to say more, but she didn't. Then he noticed the orb sitting in the middle of the coffee table. He swore to himself. Up to that point he had hoped his suspicions were wrong.

Pointing to the orb he asked, "Where did you find that?"

"Upstairs in one of the bedrooms."

He looked at her, and then sarcastically said, "so are you going to tell me what went on while I was gone. I worried about you being out here all night, and then when I come back I find you with a nasty bruise on your head, and you have nothing to say?"

Suddenly, in frustration, he slammed his coffee cup on the table. "I'm out of here. I don't need this crap in my life. Go change your clothes, and do whatever you girls do, and I'll take you back to town in time to catch the train. I'll sell this place and send you the money." He got up and began walking toward the open doorway

"Wait," Melanie called out in a small voice "please don't leave, I'll try and explain," and then she started to cry.

He turned around over and sat down beside her. "Tell me," he said gently.

In halting words she told him about finding the orb and what she had seen. "I must have bumped my head when the chair fell over."

Melanie was shaking like a leaf when she finished talking. Laying her head against his shoulder she confessed, "Sometimes I see things."

"What kinds of things," he replied calmly.

"Sometimes I will see somebody and know what is going to happen to them, or else know something they haven't told me about – like the newspaper."

"What about the newspaper?"

"Do I look like the kind of person who usually reads newspapers? Once in a while I buy the gossip rags, but the day I saw Gram's funeral announcement I had a gut feeling I needed to buy that paper. I used part of my lunch money to do it."

Adam sighed; this wasn't something he wanted to hear. Was this proof that she was a Seer?

"Does this happen very often?" He asked.

"Buying newspaper because of a feeling? First time ever."

Changing the subject he asked, "When did you eat last? I brought a few groceries for you."

"I had a bowl of soup and biscuits after you left last night."

"Go get ready. I'm taking you into town for breakfast. Besides," he added, picking up the orb, "this needs to be put into a safe place for now."

"Do you know what it is?" asked Melanie.

"I think so," he replied cautiously. *According to the ancient story, if the orbs were in play, someone is going to come looking for them. It is safer for Melanie if this is locked up in the big black safe in my office – actually its better for all of us,* he thought.

When they got to the edge of town, he stopped at a fast food drive-in and ordered their idea of a breakfast sandwich, and then drove to his office

Somehow, while juggling the orb, the bag of food, and the key, he got the door unlocked and held it open for Melanie. He led her to his office and motioned for her to sit on the sofa.

"Stay there, I'll be right back."

Melanie stared straight ahead, still slightly dazed from her experience. It seemed like only minutes passed until Adam returned with two steaming cups of coffee. He put them on the table in front of her, then opened the bag of sandwiches and handed her one.

"Eat," he said biting into his.

Melanie left hers sitting on the table "I'm not hungry. If this is your idea of taking me out for breakfast, I would hate to see where you take a girl for supper."

"Eat it anyway," he growled, "you look like you could use a few good meals."

At five feet one inch and one hundred pounds Melanie appeared gaunt. After paying for her rent and transportation each month, she had little of her income left for food and other necessities. She was used to ignoring her hunger pangs.

Once she finished eating, Adam gathered up the wrappers and put them into the garbage can beside his desk. Then he left, and returned a short time later with an insulated carafe of coffee and refilled their cups.

"Wait here," he said again, and disappeared through a small door on the other side of his office. When he returned he was carrying a wooden box. Placing it on the coffee table he picked up the orb, and began tossing it from hand to hand.

Melanie sat there waiting for him to speak. He took a deep breath, opened the wooden box and pulled out the jeweled encrusted case inside

Melanie gasped, "It's beautiful, what is it?"

He opened the case and reverently placed the orb inside. Melanie could see the case contained a large orb in the center and room for two more smaller ones. She stared at him, wondering what was going on

He returned her stare; *those blue-green eyes and cinnamon colored hair make me wish I didn't have to do this. Once I tell her the truth, her life will be changed.*

Clearing his throat he said, "Melanie right now you have two choices. You can pretend that you never found this, get on the train, go back home and forget about all of this," he said, pointing to the orb. "I will sell the land and send you the money."

"Or what," she replied, staring at him

"If I tell you about this." he replied, "your life will never be the same. You must understand that everything you knew, or had before will be gone."

Melanie was quiet for a few seconds, "You are scaring me. Does this involve my grandmother?"

"Yes."

"Then you better tell me."

Taking a deep breathe he began, "your grandmother was a rare gifted person – descended from an ancient line of mystics known as Seers. This unique ability passes from firstborn daughter to firstborn daughter.

Seers have the ability to see what is going to happen in the future. They can't change events, but can predict what will happen if a certain action takes place.

They must have custody of the orbs to be able to do this. Their responsibility is to protect the orbs, and have done so as far back as anyone can remember."

"You've got to be kidding me," Melanie exclaimed, "You believe that story?"

"Let me continue. The Seer and orbs have a value that puts them in constant danger. Again from the ancient times, there is an element in society who wants to rule the world. The catch is they must control the orbs and the Seer at the same time. One, without the other, is worthless."

Then looking directly into her eyes he said, "your grandmother was a Seer. Your mother probably was too, and it is quite likely that you are also. That is why your grandmother and mother agreed to take you away from here and cut off all communication. That is also the reason your grandmother didn't take you when your parents died.

She was trying to protect you. Your grandmother had possession of all of the orbs. She had the three of them at her home, and the one in the jeweled case was in the lead-lined safe here in the office. The role of Seer would have ended with your grandmother if you hadn't shown up at the funeral."

Melanie started to laugh, "Do you really expect me to believe this nonsense? That is a craziest story I have ever heard."

"It's the truth," he said defensively. He got up and began prowling the room trying desperately to keep his anger in check. Then he stomped back to her and sat down again "I haven't finished yet."

"This story keeps getting better and better," Melanie replied sarcastically

"In ancient times a line of men was also born. The first born son of these men was trained from early in their life to protect the Seer and orbs to their death. They were known as Sentinels. My father was your grandmother's Sentinel for many years. He looked after her, and by rite of passage I am yours."

"What?" Melanie explained, "You have to look after me? I don't think so. I have been looking after myself since I was sixteen years old, and I don't need your help."

"Yes, until the last orb is found and reunited with the others, I am stuck to you like glue."

"Even if I don't want any part of it?"

"Yeah, like I said, you have two choices, go home and forget about all of this and trust me to look after your financial interests, or find the other two and be stuck with me. I wish you had stayed where you were. Now my life is pretty well screwed up too. Like it or not, this is the way it is, until we decide what to do about the orbs."

Picking up the orb from the case and holding it as though to throw it Melanie retorted, "there is no way in hell I want to have this for the rest of my life – seeing things that are going to happen and not being able to do anything about it. I want my life back."

Taking the orb from her hand Adam placed it back into the jeweled case "I know exactly what you mean, there is no way in hell I want to spend my life looking after a little witch like you" Fixing his glare on Melanie, he said, "the sad thing is that neither of us have a choice, this is what we are born to do."

"Well I'm not – put that in your pipe and smoke it."

She turned away so he wouldn't see the angry tears in her eyes. She was determined not to cry in front of him. *I had no idea that when I saw the obituary the paper that my life was going to be turned upside down. If I had, I wouldn't have come.* Adam came up behind her put his hand on her shoulder turning her towards him.

She looked up at him, "please make this go away. I want to go home and be who I was Melanie Cain – future florist."

He looked down at her. "We don't choose how we are born. I have known all my life I was to be a Sentinel, the only thing I didn't know was for whom. I can't even begin to imagine how you must feel – how strange all of this must be for you. Now, you have to accept the fact that it is what it is, and cannot be changed."

"I know," she replied, "but I don't want it to be. I wish my mother and grandmother would have explained this to me. Things could have been so different."

Adam didn't know what to say. Awkwardly he patted her on the shoulder "maybe I should pour us another cup of coffee."

Chapter Nine

"If there are four orbs," Melanie asked "where are the other two?"

"I don't know, I assume they are here in the house some place."

"Did my grandmother have all three of the smaller ones?"

"I honestly don't know."

"Or is it that you know, and don't want to tell me?"

"Look Melanie, the best advice I can give you is to forget about all of this. Go back where you came from. All you are doing is stirring up trouble."

"Are they in the house," Melanie demanded to know, but he refused to answer.

Standing in front of him defiantly, her hands on her hips she said "I would like to get back to my house now."

"What will you do if I refuse," he replied angrily.

"Then I will walk." Picking her purse up off the floor she headed for the door.

He grabbed her by the arm and pulled her back, "no way, it is more than a freaking mile. I can't let you walk that far."

"Then drive me back like I asked."

Adam shook his head and muttered something under his breath about stubborn stupid women, "On one condition."

"What's that?"

"You don't go searching for any of the other orbs unless I am there with you."

"I really can't see what difference you being here will make. I survived finding this one." Then holding her hands open in front of him she said, "Okay, okay, I get your point," her voice dripping with sarcasm.

Adam picked up the jeweled case, put it back into the wooden box and returned it to his safe. When they arrived back at the house Melanie asked him, "would you like to come in? You can help show me around and explain what I am seeing."

The first place they went into was one of the darkened rooms Melanie had hesitated to explore the night before. Adam opened the heavy drapes and let the daylight in. Dust motes danced in the sunlight.

With Adam on one end, and Melanie on the other, they carefully removed and folded the dust covers from the furniture. Now the strange shapes from the night before began to make sense.

This room was a dining room with a long rectangular table in the center. By the time they finished uncovering the furniture there were eighteen chairs, which fit around the long table. Along one wall was a sideboard with a large tarnished silver tea service sitting on top

When Melanie opened the doors to the sideboard it was filled with English China, crystal bowls and serving dishes. Opening one of the drawers, she found it full of tarnished silver utensils, a complete six place setting for twenty-four people. Another revealed yellowed linen napkins, matching table cloths, and silver napkin holders.

Removing the dust covers on the other side of the room revealed a glass covered bar, and shelves filled with crystal glasses of all shapes and sizes, neatly lined up in rows.

"Oh my God," she exclaimed. Looking at Adam she asked, "What am I supposed to do with all of this? There's a fortune in crystal alone, never mind anything else. I can picture this huge table set, bouquets of flowers in the center, and people in fancy dresses all sitting down to eat. Behind them are servants waiting to fill the glasses with wine."

"You read too many romance novels. I'll send somebody from town to clean this room and inventory its contents. We need to know what's in here and their value for insurance purposes."

"There you go, acting all stuffy again. Let's go to the other room. I can hardly wait to see what's in there. This is so exciting," she said, dancing in front of him. "I wonder where grandma got all of this stuff, and if she ever used it?"

"This has been the family home for years so most of it was probably passed down to her."

The two of them entered the second room. To Melanie it felt more sinister than the first. Adam opened the heavily brocaded curtains to reveal a large double window. Sunlight poured into the room.

"What do you think is in here?" Melanie asked.

"There is only one way to find out," Adam replied, "Come and help me fold these."

Once all of the dust covers were removed Melanie saw this was a very masculine room. "I wonder if this was my grandfather's study?" she asked,

In one corner was a very large mahogany desk and chair. Behind the desk was a bookcase filled with hundreds of books all neatly lined up, according to size. A locked, four drawer filing cabinet looked out of place in the room.

A large stone fireplace took up another wall. A tray with a crystal liquor decanter and several crystal glasses decorated the mantle. Above the fireplace was the head of a stuffed deer. An end table with a lamp sat beside a green tweed chair. Another chair sat across from it. Melanie noticed a pipe stand with two old, well chewed pipes sitting on the table. A black bear skin rug, complete with head and glass eyes, stared at her from the floor in front of the fireplace.

Tucked into one corner was a glass gun rack containing several rifles and a shot gun. Several smaller animal heads decorated the walls. Every available space was filled with souvenirs from faraway places.

"Whoever lived here must have travelled a great deal," Melanie commented, trying to take in the room.

"Did you know your grandfather?" Adam asked.

"No, he died before I was born. Mother didn't talk much about her family after grandmother sent us away."

Always practical, Adam looked around the room and said "I am glad it's you and not me who has to deal with this. What are you going to do with it all," he said, sweeping his arm around the room. "I'm sure it meant a lot to your grandmother, but to me it looks like junk"

Melanie ignored his last comment. "I have no idea. Just being in this room gives me the creeps."

Chapter Ten

As soon as Adam left Melanie locked the front door behind him. Then she got the key ring from the kitchen, went upstairs and unlocked the second bedroom door. *I have to know if the other two are here, and if they also tell a story.* This room was almost exactly the same as the first. It took a while, but she finally found the orb hidden between the box spring and mattress.

This time she was prepared. Without disturbing the dust too much, she carried the orb down to the parlor and gently placed it on the coffee table. Once again, she dampened a soft cloth and began polishing it. Her hands were shaking; her experience with the first orb had been traumatic.

Do I really want to do this again? She thought, but curiosity was getting the best of her. Soon the orb began to hum, and then glow stronger and stronger. Just as before, Melanie's world went black. She was inside the orb, watching the drama unfold before her.

At first she felt disoriented, unsure of what she was seeing. There were two cities within a few miles of each other, yet both looked very different.

One city looked normal, older men and women walking and talking in the marketplace, women cooking meals, some sweeping the street in front of their houses. She noticed the absence of young men, which seemed strange. There were very young boys and old men.

The other city was the opposite. Soldiers sat in taverns drinking, being loud and obnoxious. Drunken men roamed the streets, the women and girls cowered in their homes. Instead of women serving in the taverns, there were young boys, some as young as ten. Some sat on the knees of the patrons, looking embarrassed as the older men fondled them.

She watched as an inebriated soldier grabbed one of the serving boys and dragged him outside. The boy was begging to be left alone, but the soldier ignored him. Outside the boy tried to run away, but the soldier caught him. Dragging the boy over to the stump of a tree, he forced the boy to bend over, rammed himself inside the child, pounding at him until he was finished. The child was screaming, snd begging for mercy.

When the soldier finished buttoning up his pants he gave the boy a coin. "Stop sniveling and get back to work. You aren't hurt. No doubt I'm only the first you will service before the night is over."

Melanie was beside herself with anger. *What kind of a place is this?*

"Feel better now," Altonio, a captain in the Army, asked the soldier when he came back into the tavern still adjusting the front of his pants.

The soldier laughed "I prefer them young and innocent. It's even better if I am their first."

Altonio asked "which one is he? Maybe I'll give him a try later, I like to feel them squirm."

Melanie grew angrier and angrier, yet there was nothing she could do. Hopelessly she watched as days blurred past, each day the same as the last – in one city men drunkenly abusing boys, in the other the normalcy of life.

Then the picture stopped and changed. Antonio and his escort of soldiers rode down the road and entered the city gates of Camorra. The women ran and hid. The guards laughed amongst themselves. They knew Antonio would stand by and watch as they abused the women the same as the boys.

Altonio rode through the city until he came to a white adobe house. Stopping outside, he bellowed, "Lot, get out here."

A man in his forties came outside. "What do you want? You have no business here."

"I've heard stories that your stepdaughter is a Seer like your wife. As you are aware, I have used her many times," he added cruelly, "I've come to see if the same is true about her daughter?"

"No it isn't," Lot lied. "I don't know where you heard such a story."

"Bring her out here so I can find out for myself." Lot realized Altonio and his men were drunk.

"You can't stop me if I demand she come with me, or I take her."

"She isn't here; she is at her aunts helping with the children."

"Can she read the orbs like her mother, who, by the way, is most enjoyable in my bed?"

"What you hear isn't true." He knew the horrors his wife had been subjected to, and he wasn't going to allow his stepdaughter, who was barely fourteen and still a virgin, to be used the same way.

Altonio pulled out his sword and touched Lot's throat with the tip. "You will bring her and the orbs to me tomorrow night. If you don't, I will come back here and use her in front of you, and I will give your wife to my men. Do you understand?"

"Yes I will do as you say – tomorrow night just as the sun goes down."

Altonio sneered at him, "Just as I thought, you really are a coward. It will please me very much to have your wife and daughter both serve me. With that I will be invincible." Altonio spurred his horse and rode away. Lot heard him laughing as he rode down the street..

He went back into his house where his wife and her daughter cowered behind the door. His stepdaughter, Leah, was sobbing as her mother tried to comfort her.

"What are we going to do?" his wife asked. "you cannot give my daughter to him. He will do terrible things to her. If we don't, he will come back, kill us and take her anyway."

"Let me think," Lot said, gathering the frightened women into his arms

That night as he slept Lot had a dream. "Take only what you can carry, but give the orbs to Leah to carry. You must leave before sunrise, and whatever you do, don't look behind you. I will lead you to a cave in the hills where you will be safe."

In the early hours before dawn Lot woke his wife and stepdaughter. "We must leave," he said, "take only what you can carry. Leah, you carry the box with the orbs wrapped in your clothing."

"Altonio will search until find us," his wife whimpered

"We have no choice," Lot replied. "Would you rather see Leah suffer the same abuse you have. Would you wish to be in the same room, and be unable to help her? This is all I can think of to save both of you."

Undetected by the guards Lot, his wife and stepdaughter, slipped through the city gates into the desert night

Once they were far away from the city Lot told them. "I had a dream last night. We are going to move into a cave in the hills where we will be safe. I was told that under no circumstances should we look back, no matter what we hear. Come, we need to hurry before someone notices we are missing." The three of them set off walking as quickly as they could toward the hills in the distance.

Daybreak came and went, the day became as black as night, and still they walked. The wind began to howl, and lightning flashed across the sky. Lot and his family found a sand dune and hid behind it, covering their faces to escape the blowing sand. The storm lasted for hours and then, as quickly as it came, it was gone. Lot heard the screams of people and animals carried on the breeze.

"Come, we must hurry. Keep going, don't look back," he reminded his wife and stepdaughter "whatever happened back there has nothing to do with us. We must keep going."

Lot's wife stopped. "I must go back. My family and friends... I need to know what happened to them."

Before Lot could stop her she turned around and cried out "it's all gone." and fell to the ground. Lot ran back to her, but saw she was dead. He grabbed Leah by the hand and began running forward chanting, "Don't look back, don't look back."

It was late evening by the time they arrived at the cave. Lot gathered a few sticks and made a small fire. They hadn't eaten all day, and drank very little. Lot opened his pack and they ate leftover honey cakes and drank from the goat skins they carried. Neither of them spoke about what had happened. It was as though talking would be too much to bear. Both fell into an exhausted restless sleep.

The next morning Lot stood on the hillside and saw that both of the two great cities had been destroyed. He watched for a long time, but didn't see any people wandering in the desert.

The two of them remained in the cave, believing they were among the last people living on earth, and wondering why they had been spared. Upon their arrival, Leah had hidden the orbs at the back of the cave, and in their struggle for survival, forgot about them.

In their sorrow and angst, they turned to each other for comfort, and in time Leah became pregnant. When she realized she was with child, she was filled with despair. If they were found she would be dragged to the nearest town, stripped naked, and stoned to death.in the town square. Her stepfather would be forced to throw the first stone. Even if she tried to hide, the men would look until they found her.

One night, in her sleep, a voice came to her. "Do not be ashamed. It is necessary Leah. There are no men here, and it is important that the line of Seer continue. Do not be afraid, and do not worry, all will be well."

Several days later Leah was at the spring getting water when a shadow fell upon her. Startled she turned around and a young man in shepherd's clothing stood watching her.

She jumped to her feet, but before she could run away, he said "I will not hurt you. Do not be afraid. I am here to protect you. I have been searching for you, and your father, for very long time."

She put her hand to her mouth, but no screams came out. She stared at him and he stared back at her. For some strange unknown reason she trusted him.

"Take me to your father. I have much to say to him." Then he added, "I know about the child, do not be afraid."

Leah led him back to the cave. Lot didn't seem surprised to see the other man. "I have been expecting you," he said quietly. The two men went outside and spoke for a long time, and then the man walked away

Leah ran to her father's side, "what did he want? What did he tell you?"

Her father looked at her sadly. "Altonio and a few of his men survived. They were out of the city on field maneuvers when they fell fell. He knows you are a Seer, knows you are alive and is looking for you. The young man has known who we are for long time and has been watching over us. He came today to warn me. In the morning we must leave this place."

But, in the morning, it was too late. When they stepped out of the cave Altonio was waiting for them. Lot put up a fight to protect his stepdaughter and his unborn child, but without a weapon he was easily defeated. Altonio stabbed him in the neck and Lot fell dead at Leah's feet.

She knelt beside him crying. "He was an old man. Why did you have to kill him? He couldn't hurt you."

Altonio reached down from his horse, scooped her up by the waist, and sat her on the horse in front of him. "It is you I came for."

Leah didn't see the man who had sworn to protect them standing on a nearby hill watching, nor did she see him following Altonio and his men as they rode away.

Altonio rode first North and then West for a full day, stopping once to eat. Leah mourned the loss of her stepfather, and was afraid that the constant jostling of the horse would cause her to lose the baby. By the time evening came, she was drifting in and out of consciousness – her mind, body, and spirit were numb. She wished she had died with her stepfather, but only the fact that she was pregnant kept her wanting to live. Altonio didn't say a word to her during their ride.

At last they arrived at a large military encampment located beside an oasis. Altonio rode up to the front of a large white tent with three spires. He jumped off his horse, then reached up and roughly pulled her down. Leah's knees buckled as her feet touched the ground. Altonio pulled her to her feet.

"Get inside," he said harshly, "and keep your mouth shut until you are spoken to."

He shoved her into the tent and she gasped at the luxury inside. Opulent rugs lay on the floor, wall hangings of silver and gold hung along the sides. At the far end was a sleeping mat filled with pillows of the richest colors and fabrics. A table with golden wine goblets was set to one side, and two young servant girls kneeled at the side of it.

To one he said "she stinks – give her a bath and some clean clothes, and then bring her back here. To the other he said, "I also need a bath. You may help me scrub my back." The young girl turned pale.

Leah was taken to a different tent, stripped of her filthy clothing, and scrubbed not too gently by the young girl. She was grateful to have her hair washed.

In a partitioned room off to one side she could hear Altonio abusing and using the other young servant girl. The young girl who washed her had tears streaming down her face and jumped each time there was a slap or scream. Leah felt sorry for both of them. Instinctively, she knew she would receive the same treatment or worse. Finally, she heard him cry out, and then the only sound was the weeping of the girl.

Once she was clothed, she was led back into the tent. Altonio was reclining on pillows holding a wine goblet, looking very smug and satisfied. The servant girl trembled as she sat at his feet, trembling, her face was streaked from her tears.

"Get us some food, I am hungry and have worked up an appetite," he said reaching over and fondling the young girl. Leah looked away disgusted. The two girls scurried out and returned shortly with two bowls of Lamb stew, a hunk of bread and a tray of fresh fruit

Pointing at Leah he commanded "eat."

"I'm not hungry."

"You will do as you're told. When I say you eat, you will eat. If I tell you to lie down and open your legs for me, you will do it."

Lea stared at him. "You are a pig."

When he didn't answer, she picked at her supper and nibbled on a piece of bread. The food stuck in her throat.

When Altonio finished eating he clapped his hands, and the servant girls removed the remnants of their meal and left.

Turning to Leah he commanded, "Stand up and remove your dress." Reluctantly she did as she was told. He walked around her, inspecting her. As he circled and touched her, he asked "are you a Seer like your mother?"

"I don't know."

"What do you mean you don't know? Didn't your mother ever tell you that you were Seer just as she was?"

"No… I don't know what you are talking about."

Running his hand down her back and between her legs Altonio tried another tactic. "Leah, did you ever see the glass orbs that your mother had?"

She felt sick to her stomach. Now she knew what Altonio wanted from her. She did have the sight, just as her mother did, and she had been trained in use of the orbs since she was a little girl.

"I don't know what you are talking about," she uttered again.

He slapped her across the face. "Where are the orbs?' he demanded.

"I don't know," she replied.

He grabbed her and threw her onto the mat. "Did you hear my serving girl screaming and pleading? I made sure you heard what I did to her. For you, it will be a hundred times worse."

Leah looked at him and calmly replied, "You will not hurt me. I am expecting a child. If I am a Seer like you think, and you cause my death and that of my baby, you will end up with nothing. There is no other who can take my place. Are you ready to risk that? Now release me."

Altonio was furious. He didn't know whether to believe her or not. If what she said was true then he couldn't take the risk.

"Tell me," he said, pulling her to her feet by her hair, and shaking her, "where are the orbs?"

Leah turned her head, refusing to speak or look at him. She spit at his feet. Grabbing her by one arm he threw her naked into a far corner of the tent. He tied her wrists together around a tent pole, and then stormed out.

"Make sure she doesn't escape," he shouted at one of the guards posted outside the entrance.

Leah was too tired to care about what was happening to her. She slid her arms to the bottom of the tent pole, curled her body around it, and fell into a troubled sleep.

Days passed and he didn't release her. She ate what little food she was given- the same way a dog would eat. She was forced to urinate and defecate into a chamber pot which was emptied daily. Every day Altonio came to her demanding to know where the orbs were. When she replied she didn't know, he struck her across the face or hit her across the back with a short whip.

During this time, the young man who had followed Leah from the cave infiltrated the camp, first as a shepherd, and later as a guard. He scouted the area and found where she was being held. He became friendly with Altonio's personal guards by supplying them with wine and losing at dice. When travelling caravans stopped at the Oasis to rest, he stole articles of men's clothing from the wash lines. Patiently he watched and waited for the right time to rescue her.

Finally that day arrived. Early one morning he watched as Altonio left accompanied by his personal guards. Unseen he slipped into the tent.

"Hush," he said to Leah when she saw him. "I have come to get you out of here."

He reached for the knife hidden in his pocket, cut the ties binding her wrists, and helped her to her feet. She was barely able to stand, and was embarrassed by her nakedness and filthy condition.

"Here," he said, "put these on and pretend you are a man. Did he touch you?" he asked as he helped her dress in the stolen clothes. Then he used the knife to cut a slit in the back of the tent.

"If you are asking did he rape me? No he didn't."

"Can you walk?" He whispered.

"Just barely."

"We will slip out the back of the tent, and then I want you to stagger like you are drunk. I will hold you up."

First he slipped through the slit he had made, checking first to see if anybody was around. When he was sure the way was clear, he led Leah out. She staggered naturally, her legs barely holding her up after not being used for so long. The young man swore and berated her as they made their way past the guards.

"You drunken fool. You are lucky I found you instead of Altonio. Do you have any idea what he would have done to you?"

Leah walked with one arm draped across his shoulder. His arm, across her back, supported her as they stumbled forward.

He led her to the back of a caravan preparing to leave, and they joined the crowd of camp followers who usually trailed behind. Once the camp disappeared from view he led her toward a nearby the hill and into a small cave he had prepared ahead of time. There he attended to the abrasions on her wrists from the ties, helped wash her body, and get dressed again. She slept while he kept watch. When night came, they left.

Several times they saw groups Altonio's guards ride past. Both knew they were looking for her.

After one such group past them Leah whispered "what if they find me?"

"They won't. As your Sentinel it is my duty to protect you, with my life if necessary."

They travelled by night and hid by day. The third morning they arrived at the cave. The body of her father was gone.

"I buried him before I followed you. See if you can find the orbs, and when night comes we will disappear. I will take you to a place where you will be safe"

Melanie came to then. She was still sitting on the sofa, clutching the orb in her hand and crying. *I don't want any of this* she sobbed. Once again, wrapping herself in the blanket, she cried herself to sleep.

Adam felt a jolt the same as before, but stronger, "damn her I told her to wait until I was with her."

"Are you talking to me," his elderly client, Annie Barrett asked, "speak up, I can't hear you."

"Not really. Do you have any more questions today, Annie?" Every three months she came to see about her will, and every three months she left without changing a thing. "Are we good for today then?" he asked.

"Yes, but I have one more question. Who is that young lady, the stranger I see you with around town? Is she related to anybody around here?"

Adam knew he was going to have to tell her. If he didn't, she would find out anyway. He also knew she wouldn't leave until she had her answers, and he needed to see what Melanie was up to.

"She is Mattie's granddaughter. She came for her grandmother's funeral."

"I remember now. Mattie did have a daughter, but didn't they have a falling out years ago? I didn't know there was a granddaughter."

"Annie, if you don't have any more questions, I have another client arriving in a few minutes."

Annie ignored him. "Funny we never saw her around before. Is she the one who stands to inherit the place? Is she going to sell it? The ladies at the tea shop are very curious."

Adam looked at her, "Annie that is really none of your business. She's my client. You have heard of lawyer client privilege haven't you?"

"Like on the television?"

"Yes Annie, just like on television," he replied patiently.

She stood up gathering her oversized purse and cane. "You don't need to be that way; I am just curious Adam, that's all. We don't get many strangers here in town."

Adam walked with her to the front door and held it open. After she left he looked at his receptionist and muttered "nosy old Biddy," and returned to his office.

The receptionist laughed, "Bill Clark canceled his appointment. He had to go out of town on business."

"Then why don't you go home early today," Adam said. "I'll lock up. I'm going to go to Mattie's, and give Melanie some more help."

The drumming in his head forced Alex awake. He smiled knowingly. *I should be hearing from the Ancient One soon.*

Chapter Eleven

When Adam arrived, he took one look at Melanie and said, "you look like hell, what have you been up to while I was gone."

I should, she said under her breath, but to Adam she replied, "I feel like it too."

"You found the second orb, didn't you?'

"Yes."

"What part of wait until I am with you before you start looking, didn't you understand?"

Melanie looked at him. "Stop bullying me, and trying to tell me what to do. I don't like this any more than you do."

Adam looked at her more carefully. There were dark circles under her eyes and her mascara had run, leaving black streaks down her cheeks. "Look Melanie, I'm sorry. Tell me about this one."

When she was finished he said, "You need a break. I am going to the city, why don't you come with me. If you decide that you are going to stay here, you might as well pack up your flat, and tell your boss you are leaving. You owe her that much.

I have several appointments to attend so you will have plenty of time, decide what you want to do. If you find the third orb, there is no turning back. Both of us are committed to see this through to the end, whatever that may be."

"I would like that. How soon are you leaving?"

"In a few hours, can you be ready by then?"

"Yes," Melanie replied, smiling for the first time that day.

Just as he expected, Alex received a message from the Ancient One, "the orbs are in a small town called Farmington in Britain. There is still one to be found, but the girl is there."

Immediately Alex contacted Hamad, "I need you and a man you trust implicitly to do a job for me. You will need your passports and be prepared to stay until you find what you are looking for."

During the drive Melanie was quiet. *I don't know what to do – should I stay in the city or go back to grandmother's house? If I stay, will I regret my decision? Am I truly called for a different purpose than what I planned? If I leave, I will have the money from the sale of the estate, but probably still have to work. Also Adam would disappear from my life. He's not as stuffy as I thought once I got to know him.*

If I go back, what will my future be? On one hand nothing will change, on the other, everything will change. Where does my destiny truly lie?

By the time Adam stopped in front of her flat she knew what she was going to do. "I am going back with you," she said.

He rolled his eyes. "I figured as much, are you sure this is what you want?"

"No I'm not sure," she snapped at him, "but it's what I've decided."

"Today is Monday, be ready to leave early Wednesday morning. I'm not going to wait for you. If you aren't ready I will leave without you."

Melanie didn't have much to pack, mostly her clothes and a few personal keepsakes. She decided to leave the furniture for the next tenant. It wasn't much, but maybe her landlady could find a use for it. Then she walked to the flower shop to give her notice.

"I'm sorry to lose you Melanie," her boss, Amy, said after Melanie explained why she was leaving, "I wouldn't want to stay here either if I had all that waiting for me. By the way, what is this lawyer Adam Brighton like?"

Melanie laughed, "He is a bossy, a royal pain in the ass, but he has been very good to me. I wouldn't have known what to do without him."

Wednesday morning she was up early and waiting when Adam drove up. He grumbled the whole time he was loading her things into his car, something about not having enough room in his sports car, and women needing to bring everything except the kitchen sink.

Chapter Twelve

While they were away, Adam had arranged for the phone company to reconnect the landline to the house.. He had also hired a young woman from town, associated with the historical society, to help Melanie do an inventory of the contents of the house, and research the values for insurance purposes.

He drove out every day after his office closed, to see how they were doing. On one such visit he took Melanie aside, "there are two strangers in town asking about you. They have swarthy complexions, and are wearing black suits. They stand out like sore thumbs."

"I wonder what they want?" she replied. "I have no idea who would be looking for me?"

"I don't know either, but I don't have a good feeling about this. Be careful okay? Remember what your mother probably told you when you were a kid, don't talk to strangers."

The next morning Melanie had to go to town to run some errands. Since Adam was unavailable she drove her grandmother's old car for the first time.

She was walking down the frozen food aisle of the grocery store when two men in black suits approached her.

"Miss Melanie Cain?"

"Yes."

"My name is Hamad, and this is my associate Abram. We understand that you have in your possession two antique glass balls. We have a client who is very interested in purchasing them from you."

Melanie knew immediately they were talking about the orbs. "You have heard wrong," she replied "I don't own anything like that. Do you mind if I ask where you got this information?"

The men ignored her. "My client has authorized us to pay a very good price for them."

"Excuse me," Melanie said, "I have no idea what you are talking about." She walked away but could feel their eyes boring into her back.

Their presence bothered her. *How did they know? Where had they come from? These must be the men Adam was telling me about.*

Instead of going directly home, she went to Adam's office. She felt like she was being followed, but when she looked back, she didn't see any one. She waited until he was done with his client, and when he saw her sitting there, he was surprised.

"Melanie, it's good to see you." Then noticing the expression on her face he asked, "is something wrong?"

"I'm not sure. You know those two men you told me about, well they approached me in the grocery store, if you can imagine. They wanted to buy two antique glass balls, but I think it's the orbs they are after."

Adam felt a shudder pass through him as all of his Sentinel senses immediately came alive.

"What did you tell them?" he asked.

"That I didn't know what they were talking about."

"I wonder how they found out. Why would they come here specifically looking for you?"

"I don't know. As far as I know, you and I are the only ones who know about them."

"Where is the second orb?"

"I put it back where I found it. That was before I decided to stay."

"You go on home, and as soon as I am finished here, I'll come out. I think we should move the second one to the safe as soon as possible. I don't like the sound of this."

"Should I make supper for us?"

"Don't bother I'll bring something with me, is Chinese okay?"

As soon as he arrived at her house Adam asked Melanie, "where is the orb?"

"Upstairs, in the second bedroom."

"Go and get it. I'll lock it in my car, and when I go back to town, I'll put it in the safe with the other one. I don't like those men being in town and you out here alone. They had better stay away from you, or they will have me to deal with."

They had barely finished supper when there was a knock on the front door.

"Are you expecting anybody?"

"No."

"You answer it" Adam said "and I'll stand behind the door where I can't be seen."

When Melanie opened the door, the same two men were standing there. "We apologize for coming to your home, but we really must insist that you sell us those glass balls. We have been instructed to offer you two hundred and fifty thousand American dollars."

"That's a lot of money" Melanie replied "but I can't help you. I don't have anything like that in my possession and, I don't know where you got that idea in the first place. Now if you'll excuse me, I'm busy, please leave."

Pushing at the door, the man called Hamad tried to force his way inside. "We know better. We will come in and look for ourselves."

Just then Adam stepped out from behind the door. "If the lady says she doesn't have them, she doesn't. Now get out of here and leave her alone. If you refuse I will call the police and have you escorted off Miss Cain's property."

The two men looked at each other and began backing away. "Sorry to bother you Miss Cain. Apparently our sources was mistaken."

Adam and Melanie stood in the open door as the two men walked back to their rental car. They waited until the men were gone before going back into the house.

Adam closed the door and locked it. He wrapped his arms around Melanie, who was trembling.

"Why do you think they are being so persistent?" she asked

"Clearly they are after the orbs, but to have two won't do them much good. They need the Seer and the orbs, which means we need to find the last one and get it into the safe with the others. While I am here we should look for the third one, and then we can take it back to my office"

. Melanie went and got the keys for the upstairs rooms. Together they unlocked the third bed room door. It was identical to the other two.

They searched the room thoroughly. Adam went so far as to pull the drawers out of the dresser to see if the orbs were tucked in behind. He inspected the mattress and box spring, but they hadn't been cut or sewn. Inch by inch they inspected the floor, but there were no places to indicate a board had been lifted.

"It's not here," Melanie exclaimed, "I was so sure it would be."

"It has to be in this house someplace. Maybe we should check the other two bedrooms again"

"I don't understand the other two were easy to find."

"I don't know what to say," Adam replied, "maybe she decided to hide the third one someplace different altogether."

They went back downstairs. "I hate to leave you here alone tonight, but I must get the second orb into the safe. Make sure you keep the doors locked while I am gone."

Melanie replied "I'll be fine, they won't be back."

"How can you be so sure about that?"

"Remember I'm a Seer, There is no use having the ability if I'm not going to use it. I assure you they won't be back tonight. Go do what you have to, I'll be fine."

Melanie stood at the window of the parlor watching Adam drive way. She wasn't feeling as confident as she let him think.

She slept very little that night hearing every creak and groan from the old house. *Who are these men and why are they here? What is going to happen when I find the third orb?*

Chapter Thirteen

Adam's feelings for Melanie became conflicted. He found her easier to be around, sassy spirit and all.. His role as Sentinel was to protect Melanie at all costs, but his heart was telling him otherwise. The more time they spent together, the stronger his feelings became. *Seers and sentinels are forbidden to marry. End of story but that doesn't make my job any easier.*

Melanie was also beginning to care for Adam. For the first time, since her mother died she felt safe and protected, that somebody cared what happened to her. Once a person got passed the stodginess, he was a lot of fun.

They had fallen into the habit of Adam coming for supper two or three times a week. When he arrived that evening he carried a brown cardboard filing box into the house.

"What have you got in there?" Melanie asked.

"Feed me first if you want to find out," he teased.

"Stop teasing and tell me, is there more of my grandmother's stuff in there?"

"You are going to have to wait and see," he replied, "now tell me what's for supper?"

"Spaghetti with meat sauce, and a green salad."

"Again? We had that the other day. Is that all you know how to make?" he grinned.

"Next time it's your turn to cook, and I don't mean bringing take-out either. If this is such a special evening, maybe we should eat in the formal dining room?"

"No, the kitchen will do just fine thank you."

After they finished eating they moved to the parlor. Melanie sat on the sofa and Adam sat down beside her, placing the box on the coffee table in front of them.

"Did I ever tell you what a good cook you are?"

"Stop stalling and show me what's in the box."

Lifting off the lid he reached in and pulled out a package of envelopes tied together with a red ribbon. "Your mom wrote your grandmother as regular as clockwork until the day she died. Your grandmother kept all of the letters."

Melanie took them from his hand. Even after all these years she recognized her mother's handwriting. "I don't understand."

"Wait, there is more."

Then he brought out another package of letters held together with a heavy red rubber band. "Your grandmother always knew where you were, and corresponded regularly with your foster parents and your social worker. These letters are more formal, and she was aware how difficult your life was. These letters stop when you left foster care.

She often talked to my father, wondering if she had made the right decision. She didn't want you to have to live the way she did, always afraid, always wondering if today was the day someone would come after her and the orbs.. She did what she thought was necessary to protect you and your mother from danger."

Pulling a small photograph album from the box, he handed it to her. "Your mother, and then your foster parents sent her pictures at regular intervals, and she kept them in here."

Melanie looked at him with tears in her eyes. "I didn't know any of this."

"I know," Adam replied, "but first you need to believe she loved you. Her instructions were quite specific. If you didn't show up at the funeral, then I was to destroy all of this and that would be then end of it. If you did, then I was to give you this box and try to explain as best I could. She loved you Melanie, and her deepest wish for you was to be happy and live a normal life."

Melanie sat there clutching photo album to her chest. "You could have kept all of this for me, yet, you didn't. Why?"

"Because you seem so lost, so alone, and I felt it was important that you knew your grandmother had this packed away. There is one more thing." He reached back into the box and pulled out a sealed letter with her name on it. "I am going to leave now and let you read your letter in private."

"You don't have to."

"Yes I do. This is a lot to handle, and I think I know you well enough to understand that you would rather be alone. I'll let myself out okay? Call me if you need me." He pulled her into his arms and kissed the top of her head, "I am here for you, and you know that."

After Adam left Melanie returned to the parlor and began reading the letters from her mother first. Each small detail of their life was in there. She giggled as remembered a few of the incidents her mother wrote about.

After her parents died the tone of the next package of letters changed. Some were from social services informing her grandmother that she had been moved again. Other letters were from her various foster parents. She saw that from an early age she had been a handful, not easy to look after. The last letter stated she had left the foster care system and had left no forwarding address. *I wonder what grandmother thought after that.*

Then she looked through the photo album. There weren't a lot of pictures, but her grandmother had written in white pencil on the black paper where she was living, the date and what the pictures represented.

When she was finished she sat there for a long time looking at the sealed envelope, not sure if she wanted to open it or not. *If I don't open it, I will never know what it contains. If I do, I may read that she was only doing her duty and never cared for me at all.*

Finally, filled with trepidation, she used two fingers to open the flap, and pulled out the single sheet of paper

My Dear Sweet Melanie,

If you are reading this letter, then I have passed away. I'm so sorry for the hardships that you have endured in your short life. How I wish I had made a different decision.

Hidden in the house are three glass orbs. Find all three and give them to Adam Brighton to take care of. He will lock them in his safe and then I want you to forget they are there. Adam is a man you can trust and he is fully aware of what he has to do.

Although you may not understand, you are descended from a long line of mystics known as Seers. This gives you the ability to see the future, and there are many in the world with devious intentions who would use this to their advantage.

The orbs alone or you alone, have no value, but if you keep the orbs in your possession you are very valuable and very vulnerable.

I am sorry for all that has happened. Your mother was Seer, and at a very early age I could see that you were too. I realize now I was wrong to have kept you both unaware of your special gifts, but all I wanted to do was protect you and your mother. I wanted you to be safe. That's why I sent you away and avoided any contact. How foolish of me.

When your mother died, I decided it would be best not to bring you here to live with me. I wanted to spare you from any possible danger, but now I realize I was wrong. Please forgive me?

I wish I had done things differently, taken you in, looked after you and shared my love with you. Now it is too late.

Trust Adam Brighton. He is your protector, just as his grandfather was mine. I love you with all my heart.

Gram

Melanie was openly sobbing by the time she finished reading the letter. Now she understood what her grandmother had done, and why her she had done what she did, but she grieved for the time they could have shared together. Melanie cried herself to sleep, clutching the letter to her heart.

Chapter Fourteen

Adam was back early the next morning, pounding on her door. When she opened it he saw her eyes were red and swollen from crying.

"I was worried about you," he said. "I brought a peace offering," holding up a tray with two large coffees and a bag of donuts.

Melanie smiled affectionately "come in you big oaf."

As they were drinking their coffee Melanie handed him her grandmother's letter to read.

"Are you sure? This is very personal."

"Go ahead, she mentions you."

When he was finished reading the letter he sat there quietly, and then asked, "Do you trust me?"

"Yes," she replied "with my life. If my grandmother says you are a good guy you must be. By the sounds of it she didn't trust too many people."

Their eyes met and held. "With my life," Melanie repeated softly

Adam looked away. *How am I going to keep my role as sentinel on a professional level if I allow myself to care too deeply for Melanie? Right now all I want to do is grab her and kiss her until she begs for mercy.*

"I have to find the other orb Adam," Melanie said.

"No you don't," he replied angrily. "Why can't you leave these things alone as they are right now? Forget about this Seer business, and live a normal life here, in this town, with me. You are safe here."

"I know you read what my grandmother wants. She expects me to find the orbs and put them into your safe."

"No! I am telling you right now to leave well enough alone. We don't know what kind of trouble those damn things could bring," he shouted at her, his hands balled into fists at his side.

Then Melanie became angry "Don't you dare shout at me, and don't you dare to presume you can tell me what to do. Just who do you think you are? I have been looking after myself since I was sixteen years old, and I've done a pretty good job so far."

The argument was on, two equally strong personalities lashing out at each other, both determined to win. Finally Adam stood up and stalked toward the door, "go ahead and do what you want, but don't expect me to help you if you get in over your head."

Slamming the door behind him, Adam walked out to his car and drove away, leaving a trail of dust hanging in the air.

Melanie went outside and stood on the top step watching him leave. When his tail lights disappeared, she closed the door. She hadn't meant to blow up at him like that, but sometimes he made her mad. *I guess if I'm going to find the third orb I might as well start looking for it. He'll be back once he cools down.*

Once again Melanie searched the third locked room upstairs, but there was nothing to be found. Two days later she had searched every nook and cranny upstairs, as well as the attic and the cellar. That left the rooms on the ground floor, but what bothered her more was that she still hadn't heard from Adam

She knew the orb wasn't in the dining room because they would have found it when they were doing inventory and cataloging the contents. She searched every inch of the kitchen, the bedroom and bathroom. By now she was beginning to feel frustrated. *That leaves only one more room, and going through it will be a nightmare. There are so many knickknacks and odd spaces that I am sure I will never find it, even if it's hidden in plain view.*

For two days, stopping only to eat and sleep, Melanie searched the library, and was becoming increasingly frustrated. Not only had she failed to find the third orb, but Adam hadn't called either.

Finally the last place left to look was the bookshelf and the books. Melanie got a ladder and started at the top left-hand shelf, and one by one flipped through the pages of each book. They were dusty, and the dust made her sneeze.

Some of the books she came across were signed first editions – Ernest Hemmingway, Somerset Maugham, and other names she didn't recognize. There were several encyclopedic collections, complete with yearbooks. In the middle of the third shelf she was thrilled to come across several of her grandmother's diaries. She put them aside to read later.

She didn't expect anything different when she opened the next book. She was shocked to find the pages had been hollowed out, and nestled inside was the third orb. Backing down the ladder, Melanie took the book containing the orb and the diaries and went back into the parlor

She didn't know what to think or do. *By far the easiest thing to do would be to phone Adam and tell him I found the last orb and have him come out and get it, or make arrangements to put it into the safe with the others. But then what?*

She was beginning to realize that her grandmother must have hidden the orbs the way she had for a reason. Was she afraid of something or someone? Was it because she didn't want the responsibilities that come with them? Maybe there was something in the diaries that would help her decide what to do. Maybe they would help her understand why she and her mother had been sent away?

Making herself a cup of tea, and sitting in the corner of the sofa with a blanket wrapped around her knees, she opened the earliest dated diary and began to read.

The first pages were those written by a young girl studying to be an archaeologist – her hopes, her dreams, her doubts, and fears. Then slowly a story began to unfold.

During the break between her third year and fourth year of studies her grandmother, Mattie had applied for, and been accepted to work on an archaeological dig on the site of the city of Masada.

The story was about a group of Jews who left the city of Jerusalem and moved to the top of the highest mountain in the area. The Romans were systematically killing the Jews, and they had barely escaped with their lives. They built a city on a plateau on top of the mountain, and lived there, safe from marauding bandits and Roman soldiers.

.   Eventually the Romans came for them. They encircled the mountain determined to capture and kill the men, and take the women and children as slaves. Only five survived the massacre, two women, two girls and a boy. The survivors were taken to Rome and lived in captivity in a Roman temple for the rest of their lives. According to the story when the Romans finally gained entry to the city all within were dead.

Mattie sure had done her homework Melanie thought. It was evident that she had carefully researched the history of the story, but in the end nobody knew for certain what was fact or fiction. The underlying question remained, if this story is true, what happened?

Previous expeditions to the site had found remnants of buildings, shards of pottery, a Roman sword, Roman coins and various other artifacts. The expedition Mattie joined was hoping to learn more about the roman encampment which had been found at the base of the hill.

Saturday April Twenty-nine

We have strict orders to stay away from the excavation sites and are forbidden to keep anything we find. A couple of days ago one of the workers located a cave buried under a rock slide. We are all excited to find out what is in there.

My job is boring - hour after hour sifting sand through a screen to see if anything comes to light. It's hot and backbreaking work, definitely not as glamorous as I thought it would be.

The entire area is marked into a grid of three meters by three meters. Each of us is responsible for our own grid, and if we find something we call Henry Symes to come over. Henry is the head of the dig, and if he thinks what we found is of value, we have to wait until they have taken photographs and marked on a map the location where the artifact was found. Then it is taken to a large white tent, cataloged and numbered.

I haven't been lucky enough to find much in my grid, but we share in the excitement of those who have. Maybe one day it will be my turn to find something of value. Who knows, I could become famous.

Friday, May Seventh

The entrance to the cave has been cleared away. I heard they found as many as twenty-four sets of remains all huddled together in one area. The question going around the supper table was how did they get there? There is speculation that there must be some sort of opening that leads to the top of the hill. It is surprising that, after more than one thousand years, there are still identifiable bone fragments.

Everyday Mr. Symes reminds us that we are strictly forbidden to go anywhere close to the cave. I'm pretty sure he tells us the same things over and over just to hear himself talk. I am curious; I want to know what's inside.

Monday May Tenth

I think that whatever was found inside the cave must be important. There are visitors coming and going at the site. I have seen government people going in and out of the office tent. Mr. Symes is cranky, and barks about everything we do. Nothing we do is right.

May Seventeenth

They began removing crates from the cave and loading them onto trucks. We hear rumors of course, but nothing definite. I wish I could go in there to see for myself. The days are getting unbearably hot. We work in the morning until it gets too hot, and then return when it begins to cool off, and work until the sun goes down.

Thursday May Twenty-eight

For whatever reason, there is virtually no activity around the cave entrance today. They must have removed all of what was in there. I have decided that after supper I'm going to go inside and take a peek for myself. I would like to be able to say, "Yes I was there when they found that."

When I was sure there was nobody around I made my way to the cave. It was dark inside, but I didn't want to use my flashlight too much until I was far enough inside that nobody would see it.

Using the wall as a guide to help me keep from falling, I moved my flashlight around. The cave was larger than I thought it would be. As I moved my light around the floor I noticed, in the rubble of a slide, something sticking out of a pile of dirt.

Curiosity got the best of me. Despite the instructions we all received, 'don't touch anything,' I began digging out the object with my bare hands. It was a wooden chest, made from a type of wood I have never seen before. A piece of twig had been forced through the clasp to lock it.

Pulling the twig out, I opened the chest, hoping to find a treasure inside. Instead of gold there was a dirty old jewel encrusted box were three glass orbs, covered with dust, forming a circle around a larger one.

I thought I heard a noise and stopped to listen, hoping I hadn't been followed into the cave. Then I realized the sound I was hearing came from my own heavy breathing. My heart felt like it was going to jump out of my chest.

Using my shirt tail I took one of the smaller orbs from the chest, and carefully wiped the dust from it. The orb felt warm in my hand, yet the air in the cave was cold and dank. I repeated the process with the other two, and when I returned them to their places in the chest, they seemed to glow dimly.

I was afraid as I picked up the largest orb. I knew something wasn't right, but I went ahead and began removing the dust anyway.

Suddenly, a brilliant white light shot out from the largest orb onto the ceiling. The light surrounded me, lighting up the cave with its brilliance, and then disappeared.

My hands were shaking as I hurriedly closed the wooden chest, put it back where I found it, and covered it back up with dirt. I made sure it was completely covered, and prayed that nobody had seen the light display and decided to come and investigate.

I can't let anyone know what I have found. Whatever was in that box has affected me deeply. It is a feeling too powerful for me to understand.

I turned and edged my way out of the cave. I was shaking, my hands and clothes dusty from the cave. The night was dark as I made my way from the cave and back to my tent. Once again I wanted to make sure that nobody saw me, but just in case, I took a circuitous route. Everything appeared to be the same, and yet all was different

I was different. I felt different. I felt as though I was in a trance as I made my way back to my tent. *Too much sun for one day* but I knew that wasn't the reason. I couldn't comprehend what had just happened

Simeon, an English man, called out to me as I walked past him. When I stopped he approached me with a canteen in his hand. "Here, have some water. It's not good to sweat so much on such a hot day."

I hadn't seen him around camp before, but didn't think much about it. People were quitting and being hired all the time. After drinking half of the water in the canteen I asked. "Are you new here?"

"Yes ma'am," he replied, "I am here to watch over you." Then looking around to make sure no one could hear him, he whispered "you must remove what you found in the cave and hide it. Don't tell any of the others, this is just between you and me."

"How did you know? Who told you," I whispered, but he was gone.

The next night, when the camp was quiet, and everybody seemed to be asleep I made my way back to the cave. I wrapped the chest in the small blanket I had brought, and carried it to my tent.

Once safely back, I pulled out my small suitcase out from under my cot, put the chest, blanket and all in the suitcase, and then shoved it back under the cot as far as I could reach.. I knew what I was doing was wrong. If I got caught I could be charged with theft. If I tried to take the chest out of the country, I would be charged with trying to smuggle antiquities, and sent to jail for a very long time.

I laid awake for a long time, jumping at every sound I heard. Finally, I fell into a restless sleep, filled with dreams of flashing lights, and voices crying out to be heard

June 4

I am frightened. Maybe it is my guilty conscience, but I feel like someone is watching me all the time. There are rumors that there is supposed to be a treasure of great value in the cave, and it can't be found. I go about my business, doing what I have to do. Mr. Symes is getting more miserable by the day, shouting and cursing at us all the time.

June Ten

When I came back today my tent was a mess. My bed had been stripped, my clothes were strewn all over the floor, and everything had been turned upside down. My large suitcase was dumped on top of the bed.

My heart felt like it was in my throat. I was afraid that whoever had been in there might have found the suitcase under the cot. If they had, I was sure to be accused of stealing, and sent home in disgrace. I couldn't help but wonder how my father would take that.

When I was sure nobody nearby, I pulled out the suitcase, and opened it. The locked box was still there just as I had left it. I can't explain how I felt, but I knew this box was important, and I was meant to find it. Simeon has become my closest friend. He is always where I can see him, he makes me feel safe. I trust him. If he was going to report me to Mr. Symes he would've done it by now

June twenty

All hell broke loose today. Mr. Symes called me to the tent he calls his office and began questioning me.

"Mattie, you were seen going into the cave when you are strictly for bidden to do so."

I thought to myself *if what he says is true then I might as well admit it.*

"Yes," I told him, "I did go inside. I was curious to see what it looked like."

"Did you see anything unusual while you were in there?"

"No sir. In fact I was kind of disappointed, it looked like every other cave, I have seen before, but then I didn't go in very far. It was dark, and all I had was my flashlight."

"Did you do some digging in the back where the remains were?"

"No Sir. I didn't go back that far, I stayed close to the entrance."

"Mattie, I have to ask you this, and I want you to tell me the truth, did you remove something from the cave?"

"Like what?"

"A container, a sack, a box or something in that line, something you could carry out?"

"No Sir," I was lying, and I think by looking at my face he knew it. Somehow I knew this man must never have the orbs.

"Mattie, are you telling me the truth?"

"Yes sir and I resent being called in here and being accused of lying and stealing. I have been doing my job just as it was assigned to me."

Then I knew. "You had somebody search my tent didn't you? So you must know by now I have nothing to hide."

"Yes I authorized a search, and as we speak, it is being searched again."

"Why are you singling me out? Are you searching all the other tents or just mine?"

"Just yours."

"Why?"

"A valuable artifact is missing, and one of the guards saw you carry something out of the cave and take it to your tent."

I felt sick to my stomach; my father would be angry and disapprove of me if he learned of this.

"Sit down Mattie. We will wait until I find out the results of this search."

It seemed like we sat there forever. Finally a guard opened the tent flap and Mr. Symes went out to talk to him. I could hear the murmur of their voices, but couldn't make out what they were saying.

Mr. Symes came back in, "you are free to go now Mattie."

Just like that I was furious, and I told him so. I didn't care if I got fired or not.

"You bring me in here, accuse me of all kinds of things, and then dismiss me just like that. I demand to know what, if anything, did you gain by searching my tent, besides embarrassing me? I am sure everybody in the compound watched what your men were doing."

"There was nothing there. My information must have been wrong. Just in case you're tempted again, stay out of the cave. If you are seen going near there again, you will be dismissed

"Yes Sir," I said. As I was leaving his tent I actually felt like saluting him, like he was some kind of general, but didn't. I am so mad.

When I got back to my tent I cleaned up the mess. This time the small suitcase was lying on top of my cot and was empty. In a way I'm glad the box was gone, but I can't help wonder where it is.

I returned to work as if nothing happened. Instead of chatting back and forth as we usually did, the other workers looked away. At meal times I sat alone. Grave robbing is considered an unforgivable offense, and I wonder if that's what they think I was doing.

June Thirty

I went to Mr. Symes and quit. I asked him to arrange a ride to the nearest city, and from there I would find my own way home. He made no effort to ask me to stay. I said to him, "by the way before I leave, do you want to check my luggage and make sure I'm not stealing anything."

"Simeon is leaving too. You can travel with him. Good riddance to the both of you."

I couldn't help taking one more jab at him, "Are you going to check his bags too?"

"No, he wasn't in the cave. I'll have a car for you in the morning. Goodbye Mattie. I am disappointed in you, and I will be sure to let your father and your professors know why."

"You do whatever you have to do," I replied and walked out. I was seething with anger.

The next morning a hired driver took Simeon and me to the nearest town where we could get on a train. We were sitting on the platform waiting when he whispered to me. "The case with the orbs is safe. I removed it from your tent when you left that morning."

I looked surprised "why did you do that."

"Mattie, you are a Seer, and from now on, my job is to look after you. It's a good thing I showed up when I did."

I had no idea what he was talking about, but during our long train ride, he explained to me what a Seer was, and why he had to protect me. I honestly didn't know whether to believe him or not, but deep down I knew he was telling me the truth.

That was the last entry in that diary. The next entries were written after the fact, and spaced far apart.

When we arrived at the docks Simeon and I went to the booking office and bought passage on the Nightingale, which was sailing the next morning. Simeon was booked into a cabin with three other men, and my cabin contained two other women. He kept the suitcase with the orbs in his possession, his reasoning being that he was not under suspicion and I was, or had been.

From there we walked to the dock and located our ship. Because it was leaving early the next morning, we were allowed to board later in the evening. We went to have a bite to eat at a nearby inn, and then made our way back to the ship.

There was a man standing at the gang plank and Simeon went ahead to show him our tickets, and get permission to board. He motioned for me to come. As I started to move forward, a big policeman stepped in front of me.

"Are you Mattie Ashworth?" he asked me

"Yes," I replied.

"You are to come with me."

"What's wrong? Has something happened?" My first thought was of my father. Simeon stayed where he was and watched.

"You need to come with us to the police station. You are suspected of trying to smuggle valuable antiques out of the country."

I stared at him. "Are you serious?"

By this time Simeon decided to come and see what was holding me up. "What is going on here officer, I am responsible for getting this young lady safely home."

"It's okay Simeon, these gentlemen have been told I am smuggling antiquities out of the country, but we both know I have nothing to hide." I said with a calmness I didn't feel. "Obviously Mr. Symes is behind this, and didn't believe me."

"Is this all of your luggage?" The police officer asked.

"Is this really necessary?" I said. I was beginning to panic. I looked to Simeon for help, but before he could say anything, the officer took hold of my elbow and began steering me through the crowd that had gathered. A second police man struggled behind with my luggage.

"Where are you taking her?" Simeon demanded.

"Rupert Street precinct."

"Don't worry Mattie I'll be there as soon as I can."

When we arrived at the police station, I was taken into a room with no windows, a table and two wooden straight back chairs. My suitcases were opened and searched one piece at a time. They went as far as slicing the lining to be sure nothing was hidden in there.

"Wait here," the police officer said when he was finished.

I sat there for a long time. I didn't know what was going on or what was going to happen to me.. Finally he returned, "Miss. Ashworth, I have a few questions for you. Why did you leave the dig when you did? You were expected to be there for another two months."

"I was finding it difficult to stay after Mr. Symes accused me of the lying and stealing," I replied.

"Why did he accuse you?"

"One day I went into the cave they were excavating after being told not to."

"Why did you do that?"

"I was curious. I wanted to see what was in there."

"Did you remove anything from the cave?"

I looked him right in the eye and said "no I did not. Now may I leave?"

"Soon. Why would this Mr. Symes think that you had removed something?"

"I don't know."

This went on for a long time. He kept asking me the same questions over and over; I kept giving him the same answers.

There was a knock at the door, and he left the room again. When he returned he said "your friend has come to collect you. You are free to go."

Tears stung my eyes as I put my belongings back into the suitcases. I felt humiliated and angry, but I wasn't going to let him see me cry.

Simeon came into the room with a porter. "Come," he said, "let's get you out of here,". On our way back to the ship Simeon said, "I convinced the purser to change our accommodations. We are together. I told him we got married after booking our tickets."

"What? Both of us – in one cabin? I can already hear what my father will say about that."

"Yes but don't worry, you are safe with me. I won't touch you. This way I know where you are, and where the orbs are."

When our ship docked my father was waiting for me. He was furious. As soon as I saw the look on his face, I knew he had heard from Mr. Symes.

"Father..." I began to say to him, but he cut me off.

"Get in the car Mattie." Then turning to Simeon he demanded, "who are you?"

"I am Simeon Brighton, and I worked with Mattie on the Masada dig. I was asked to escort her home, and see that she arrived safely."

"Your job is done," my father said curtly.

I looked at Simeon and felt the need to apologize. "I'm sorry my father is so rude."

He looked at me, "well then I guess my job is done, see you around sometime Mattie."

He turned his back to me and walked away, taking the orbs and my suit case with him. I wondered why he was acting that way. *He must have his own reasons* I decided.

August

Father still hasn't forgiven me. He has also refused to allow me to go back to university to finish my studies. He told me that he can no longer trust me, and that I am a great disappointment to him. I am devastated, and have heard nothing from Simeon.

One year later

I couldn't believe my eyes when I saw Simeon walking on the street in town. Not thinking, I called out to him. When he saw it was me, he ran across the street, picked me up and swung me around. It was so good to see him again. A pretty dark haired lady crossed behind him and then came and stood beside him. She was obviously expecting a child.

"Mattie, allow me to introduce you to my wife Alicia. We recently purchased a small farm not too far from town."

"Alicia, this is Mattie Ashworth. We were on the Masada dig I told you about. In fact, we travelled back home at the same time."

I put out my hand and shook hers. "I am pleased to meet you." I said. To Simeon I said. "Congratulations, I am very happy for you."

We chatted a bit, and Alicia and I agreed to meet for tea the next day.

Six months later

Lloyd Allan and I are getting married. He proposed last night and I said yes. I'm not sure what father will think about this, because Lloyd isn't one of his favorite people. I am beyond happy. I don't think father would approve of the man I choose to spend my life with.

June

Simeon came to the house and brought my suitcase with him.

"I heard you are getting married," he said. "Good for you. I think it's probably safe to return these to you now. Your new husband will be here to look after you."

"What am I supposed to do with them?" I asked.

"I think it's best to hide them. Let's look around and see if we can find a good place."

We inspected all of the out buildings, and when we came to the old chicken coop he said,
"This looks like as good a place as any. Can you find me a hammer Mattie?"

I went to the barn and brought back a rusty claw hammer. He ripped up three of the floor boards, placed the suit case in the open space and nailed the boards back down. "They should be safe there."

"Mattie," he said, taking my hands in his, "if you ever need help, I am here for you."

September

I am pregnant. We have been married for three months. I can hardly wait to find out whether the baby is a boy or girl.

March

Lloyd has been called to serve in the army. I don't want him to go. I want him to stay home until the baby comes. It's only for two more months.

<u>May</u>

We have a beautiful baby girl and I have called her Barbara. I can hardly wait for Lloyd to come home and see her. I know he will love her as much as I do.

<u>September</u>

Lloyd is dead. The telegram said he was killed in action. I can't believe he is never coming home again, or that his little girl will never know her daddy. I am numb, I can't seem to function and I don't know what to do. Simeon and Alicia have been here with me, and I am grateful for their support and friendship. Father has been very quiet. He pats me on the shoulder, shakes his head and walks away.

The next entries became fewer and more general. Melanie thought there must be more about her mother and herself, but didn't want to read ahead.

<u>Years later</u>

My friend and protector Simeon passed from this earth today. He was far too young, and I will miss him terribly. I have come to rely on his friendship and steadiness. I don't know how I would have got through these years without him. I loved him for the kind, gentle, caring soul he was. Alicia is handling this very well. We both knew it was only a matter of time because he had been sick for a long time.

On his death bed, he told me as long as I have the orbs I must always be alert. He has asked his son Hugh to continue watching over me in his place. He made it sound like I can't look after myself.

Since I lost Lloyd, I have raised Barbara by myself, and feel like I have done a good job. I managed to raise her, get her married to a decent fellow, and she has made me a grandmother of a beautiful little girl called Melanie.

April

Last night I saw lights in the backyard by the outbuildings. Why would someone come into my yard? What would they want? Not so long ago I had a feeling that someone had been in the garage – a few things were out of place, but I'm not sure if anything was taken.

<u>Two weeks later</u>

When I came home from town today, I had the distinct feeling that somebody had been in my house. Nothing seems moved or displaced, but I can't shake the idea someone was in here. Maybe my old mind is playing tricks on me.

<u>June</u>

This morning I saw where someone has been digging holes by the old chicken coop. I called Hugh to come over, and for the first time we spoke about the orbs. Simeon had told him everything. When we went into the old coop we saw nothing had been disturbed but, I have a sick feeling that the orbs have something to do with all of this strange activity.

Hugh knows I am a Seer, and Simeon was the only other person who knew. I have kept this a secret from Barbara, and if Lloyd ever suspected, he didn't say a thing.

Hugh and I agree that our best course of action is to separate the orbs. He is going to dig them up for me, disguise the case in a wooden box, take the largest one to his office and put it in his safe. I am going to bring the others into the house and hide them.

I wish I wasn't cursed with this special ability. I've watched Barbara over the years and now Melanie, and I see they are also gifted. I am afraid for them.

Three weeks later

A man came to my door, who claimed to be an antique buyer. He told me he had heard in town that I had some antiques I wanted to sell. I took him out to the garage where father had stored many pieces of old furniture.

He seemed perfectly legitimate until he asked if I had ever seen a box with three glass balls. He said he had heard a story that I possess such a treasure. If I did, he was interested in buying it from me.

I froze. I immediately knew he was talking about the orbs, but how did he find out? Who would have told him that? I told him I had never seen anything like that in the garage, but that it had been years since I'd even looked at the furniture, and had no idea what was in there. If I found what he was looking for, I would definitely call him.

Now I am afraid – not so much for me, but for Barbara and Melanie. I am an old lady and they can't hurt me, but they might figure out my girls are gifted too. Hugh advised me to stick to my daily routine and not change anything. If I am being watched, changing what I do will only bring me unwanted attention.

<u>August</u>

Barbara and Melanie came to stay for a few days. My, that little girl is growing fast. I decided it was time to tell Barbara the story about the orbs. At first I don't think she believed me, but she didn't seem as surprised as I thought she would be. That's when she told me that she had known all her life that she was different from other girls, and that she was able to predict what was going to happen.

It took a bit of talking, but I finally convinced her that, for her safety and Melanie's, they should stay away for a while.

They are in danger because of me, and I couldn't stand it if something happened to one of them because of the orbs. Of course, she didn't agree and we argued, but in the end I was able to make her see it my way. We both cried when she left. I assured her this was a temporary situation and that I would write her every week.

<u>Two years later</u>

I have been meaning to keep writing in this diary, but didn't. Barbara and her husband were killed in a car accident. I was laid up with a broken leg and unable to go to the funeral. I don't know if I will ever forgive myself for that. My heart is broken, I don't know if I can survive this.

That man came around again, and has been constantly calling to see if I found the glass balls. Then he made a comment about Melanie and Barbara not coming to visit me for a long time. That really scared me. Was he keeping tabs on my coming and going?

Social services have been in contact with me, asking if I would take Melanie. God forgive me, but I said no. I must protect her from anyone who might try to hurt her. Sometimes I wonder if what happened to Barbara was really an accident.

I have never hurt so much in my life. First I send my daughter away, and then I refuse to look after my granddaughter. I just can't see where I have any other choice, but I'm not proud of what I have done. What kind of a person am I?

When Melanie finished reading the last entry she put the diary down on the coffee table. She could feel her grandmother's anguish. Now she could begin to understand the choice the old lady had made, but that still didn't make it right. *I wonder if she knew how much this hurt me*

Chapter Fifteen

Now, more than ever, Melanie was intrigued by the orbs. Were they connected to the ancient story of Masada? She googled Masada on her computer, and read the numerous accounts of the story, which, in turn fueled her imagination even more. There was a brief mention of the dig her grandmother had been on, but no real information.

She took the third orb out of the book and stared at it for a long time. *There is only one way to find out.* For the third time, she polished an orb with a soft cloth, and it began to hum and glow like the others. This time she was ready.

* * * *

As the picture became clearer, Melanie once again moved into the orb. She was in a city built high above a mountain called Masada. The first thing she noticed was that the path up the mountain was barely wide enough for one horse..

She wondered *who are these people and why are they living up here. Everything they need has to be brought up to them except water.* Somehow there was a well in the center of town.   Then she heard shouting. A young boy of about twelve years old ran into a house calling out to his mother.

"An army is coming," he shouted at her.

"Is it the raiding party coming back? They went out early this morning." Frequently the men of the city would raid caravans or military camps for extra food supplies.

"No mother, they have been back for some time."

Rebecca wiped her hands on her apron and she and her son hurried to the wall surrounding the city. There was a great cloud of dust in the distance, too much to be the usual patrol which passed once a week.

"You stay here," Rebecca said to her son. She ran back into her home. From a niche built into a corner of her bedroom she removed a jewel encrusted case containing four glass balls.. She put the open case on the table, and taking deep breaths tried to slow her racing heart. As she focused on the orbs, they began to glow, and a picture formed inside the center one.

It looked like a mighty battle had taken place; the bodies of her people lay in the streets. Roman soldiers strutted up and down, but there were no dead soldiers to be seen. Rebecca instinctively knew a few of her people had survived, but how many and who she couldn't see. When the orb went dark, she reverently put it back into the small case and put it back to where she had found it.

I must tell one of the Elders what I have seen. She ran down the street to the temple and up the stairs, pushing past a guard who tried to stop her. Then sprinting down the corridor she called out to Nemo, who was the chief priest.

"Rebecca what on earth are you making such a racket about? Everybody in town can hear you."

"Nemo, the soldiers are coming. This is the beginning of the end."

"Come in here Rebecca, and tell me what you are carrying on about" he said ushering her into a room and closing the door behind them. "Sit down and catch your breath."

Rebecca refused his offer to sit. "Nemo a great cloud of dust has been seen in the distance. I have consulted the orbs, we are lost."

Rebecca was a woman deeply respected for her ability to perceive the future. She had consulted with Nemo many times

"Stop and tell me exactly what you saw."

She told him the details of what she had seen in the orb. When she finished, Nemo called to one of the guards, "go out to the top of the walls and report back what you see."

Within minutes he returned. "She is telling the truth. By the size of the dust cloud an Army is coming this way"

Frightened, Nemo said, "Sound the signal for the Elders to come to the temple immediately."

Until they arrived Rebecca paced back and forth. The only sound was the slap of her sandals on the stone floor.

Nemo left to meet with the Elders. A short time later he returned to her and said "you must come and tell the assembly what you know."

She repeated to the gathering of men what she had seen in the orbs. Some listened carefully, becoming more and more distressed, others scoffed at her.

"What are you worried about Rebecca? We are safe up here, nobody can touch us. In order to get to the top they have to come up the path one at a time, and we can kill them as they come.

Frustrated with their lack of understanding she replied, "I know what I saw."

"How do you suppose they're going to get up here, fly like the birds?" Another scoffed.

Looking at Nemo she said, "I think we should begin to prepare for a siege, I know what is going to happen."

While they were in the temple discussing what to do, the entire city gathered around the top of the wall and watched as the Army marched closer. They waited as the army stopped in front of the mountain, surrounding it on two sides. As the Army made camp, the people noted there were thousands of soldiers on the plain below.

"How do they plan to get up here?" they asked each other.

The next day they watched as Jewish slaves packed huge timbers to the base of the mountain wall and began building a frame. Once the base of the frame was secured they began building crisscrossing walls that began to climb upward.

Sometimes the guards shot arrows and killed one of the slaves, but another took his place. The men of the city went out at night to harass the encampment and steal food and weapons. On one such excursion, they managed to set the wooden framework on fire. Rather than discouraging the soldiers, the burnt timbers were hauled away, and the slaves resumed their building.

Once again the Elders called Rebecca to the temple. "Bring your orbs and tell us what you see." Once again Rebecca consulted the orbs. Expectantly the scribes waited for her to tell them what she saw.

She looked at the group, "sadly the pictures haven't changed."

"Tell us what pictures the orbs show you? What can we do to change the result?" By now they had come to believe her original predictions.

"I don't know. All I am able to see is a result of an action. I have no way of changing the future."

They argued among themselves, but soon all realized they had no hope of defeating the Romans. They were trapped, and each day the wooden scaffold climbed higher.

The Elders knew they were defeated. They also knew the Romans would kill the men and the boys, whether they fought back or not. The women and girls would become slaves, and more than likely raped by the soldiers. They all agreed that the women and girls needed to be protected from such a terrible fate.

After meeting for a great length of time they agreed on a plan. They chose to die instead of being captured by the Romans. The Elders called the citizens to an assembly, and after listening all agreed to the plan that no one would be alive when the soldiers entered the city. Many men stepped forward declaring they would kill their family first and die with them. When the time came, ten brave men would be chosen to kill the last of the people. They would rather die than submit to Roman rule

Amos, who was a close friend of Rebecca's, came to her. "We must hide the orbs and keep you and your daughter Lana safe. We cannot allow the Romans to capture you and the orbs."

As much as Rebecca wanted to disagree with him she knew he spoke the truth. Below the mountain was a huge cave that could only be accessed by rope. Rebecca gave Amos the case containing the orbs, and helped lower him into to the cave to hide the them.

When that was done Amos set about finding a place to hide Rebecca and her two children. He convinced his wife to go with Rebecca and take their son. Rebecca was a Seer, he was her Sentinel, and both lines needed to continue.

The city watched silently the day the scaffold was finished and the workers began building a bridge toward the wall. The time had come. In the dark of night husbands and fathers kissed their wives and children one last time, and stabbed them. Then they lay down beside their family and drove the knives into their own hearts.

One small group of twenty-four shimmied down the ropes into the cave, intending to hide out until the Roman's left. Unfortunately the last man was hurt as the rope broke, plunging him to the floor below. The group hadn't expected this to happen, and had brought no food or water. Unless the Romans rescued them, they had no chance of survival.

Silence fell over the city. The ten chosen men went from house to house killing the wounded, and those who had no family. Dogs ran around the city, barking furiously, maddened by the scent of blood hanging in the air.

Amos gathered the two small families, led them to the communal bathing area, and locked them in. Then he went back home and fell upon his knife.

As soon as the breach was complete, the Roman soldiers lined up and waited their turn to climb the scaffold.

Amine would lead his soldiers across the bridge. Taking one of his Lieutenants' aside he said to him, "There is a Seer named Rebecca. When you find her, and the orbs, bring them to me. The whole point of this maneuver is to seize her. When she is in my bed, I will have the power to rule the world."

The soldiers were hesitant to enter the city. It was too quiet; they sensed that something wasn't right. Amine called three of his best men forward. "Sneak into the city and find out if the people are preparing to ambush us."

When his men returned they reported to him. "They are all dead. There is no one alive. Families lie dead in their homes"

"All of them?"

"We haven't found anybody alive yet," he replied

Amine, taking ten armed soldiers with him, began to walk through the city. Everywhere he looked he saw dead people.

How can this be? What kind of people are these to choose death over life?

When he came to the communal bath Amine saw the door was locked. His men, using a battering ram, forced it open. There in front of him were two women and three children, the sole survivors of the suicide pact.

"Take them back to my tent," he commanded "but don't hurt them. Perhaps they can help us understand what happened here."

The soldiers ransacked the city taking all of the gold, food, and weapons they could carry. Others gathered the dead bodies and moved them to the town square. There a funeral pyre was built and the bodies burned. When questioned by Amine, Rebecca gave a false name, and from then on was known as Tia.

Within two days the army had left for home. Only the scaffold and burning pyre remained to indicate the spot where thousands had died.

The captives were taken to a temple in Rome where the older women lived out their days. Their children grew, were educated as Romans, married, and the lines of Seer and Sentinel flourished

* * *

Just as quickly as she had left it, Melanie came back into the parlor. She had a massive headache and every movement made it worse. She lay there, not moving, until it disappeared.

On the other side of the world, Alex received a message from the Ancient One "all of the orbs have been found, and are in play. To have them without the Seer is of no value. You must have both in one place to achieve success."

Chapter Sixteen

Adam knew without being told Melanie had found the third orb. He had known all along that she wouldn't stop looking, and was surprised it had taken this long. He had hoped by staying away she would give up her search. *Stubborn little witch, just like her grandmother. She comes by that honestly that's for sure.*

He missed not seeing her every day, but it was the only way he could continue to protect her. *I am already in over my head, and don't have a clue what to do from here.*

Grabbing his jacket from the back of the chair, he went out to his car and broke the speed limit driving to her place. The door was unlocked when he arrived, and when he called out there was no answer. Worried he hurried into the parlor. Melanie was lying on the sofa with her arm over her eyes, pain etched in the lines on her face.

"Melanie. What happened? Are you hurt?" Then he saw the orb clutched tightly in her hand.

"You had to keep looking and until you found it. Do you even realize how much danger you are in now? Why didn't you listen and leave things as they were."

Then he noticed she was crying. Sitting down beside her on the sofa he pulled her into his arms.

"I'm sorry," she said between sobs. "It's a sad story all the way around. I know what you mean now. All these orbs have done is cause misery and pain. Even my grandmother suffered because of them."

She felt so small in his arms that he couldn't resist pulling her closer to him. She put her head on his chest, and he held her for a long time.

Just about the time he thought she had fallen asleep she looked up at him. "Can you forgive me Adam? I never meant to hurt you."

Without thinking he lowered his lips to hers and kissed her. At first she resisted then began kissing him back. Suddenly he pushed her away. "I can't do this Melanie. I can't protect you and care as much as I do. The only thing I am sure about is if your grandmother hadn't died, I wouldn't have met you."

"What do we do now Adam?"

"The first thing we need to do tonight is get this orb into the safe with the others. Then, hopefully, we can relax and breathe for a while. That will give us time to figure this out. Have you eaten today?"

"No."

"I'll go make us a sandwich, and then you can tell me how you found the orb, and what you saw. After that we'll go into town and lock this one away with the others. Maybe, with any luck, this is the end of everything."

While they ate Melanie showed him the diaries. "Now I understand what compelled grandmother to try and keep us safe, but there must have been another way, instead of sending mother and me away?"

"Things were different then Melanie. You have to remember that. There wasn't the means of communication, and women weren't as liberated as they are now. That, and the fact she was alone, afraid, and didn't have a man to protect her.

My grandfather Simeon did the best he could, but he had his own family to look after. Before he died, he told my dad the story, and begged him to watch over Mattie. When dad died, it was my turn.

I think that man coming to her door really spooked her. I remember grandfather rushing to attend her more than once. It's strange what we will do in the name of love. We just can't think straight, and my grandfather loved your grandmother."

Then switching topics he asked, "How is your headache now?"

"Nearly gone, it's much better now that I had something to eat."

"Feel up to taking this orb into town?"

"Yes, I can probably manage that," she said, smiling shyly.

They went back to Adam's office, and once again he got the wooden box out of the safe. Melanie gently placed the third orb inside the jeweled case.

"I really hope this is the end of it," she murmured.

"Me too," Adam replied as he picked the box up and carried it back to his safe."

"Now, he said, "Let's get you home so you can get a good night's sleep."

When they arrived back at the house Melanie asked him. "Can you come in for a while?"

"Don't tempt me." He gathered her in his arms and gently kissed her. "Now do you understand why I can't? This is dangerous for both of us."

He turned around and walked toward his car cursing under his breath.

Chapter Seventeen

For several weeks life fell into a normal routine. They never spoke about the orbs. Adam was still struggling between his feelings for Melanie, and his deep sense of duty. Wisely, Melanie said nothing. Adam would have to decide what was best for him.

Now when Melanie entered her home, she was relieved the orbs were no longer in the house. They were safely locked in Adam's safe and would be there for the rest of time. She went into the kitchen and put away her two bags of groceries. That reminded her; she had to go to the bank to make arrangements for the cash part of the estate. Adam had reminded her several times, but she kept forgetting. The advance he had given her was nearly gone.

She made a peanut butter and jam sandwich and a cup of tea, and carried them into the parlor. She had just put her cup of tea on the coffee table, when she heard a noise behind her. Melanie had no way of knowing the two men in black suits were inside waiting for her.

"Miss Caine…"

She froze. When she heard the voice her first thought was that she had heard that the heavily accented voice before, but she couldn't place it. Slowly she turned around to see the man she had known as Hamad standing behind her.

"How did you get in here?" she gasped

"It was easy, you forgot to lock the door, but even if you had, that wouldn't have stopped me."

Melanie was frightened. Slowly she edged around the coffee table toward the door, trying to put some distance between the two of them. "What do you want?"

"I have come for the orbs," he replied "we know you have all of them now."

"What makes you think that? I told you before that I don't know what you are talking about."

"Stop lying Miss Cain. We know different. The Ancient One told us. What we didn't understand at first was that we needed them and you."

"Well, you're out of luck. They aren't here. They have been put away in a safe place." Immediately, Melanie realized she had made a mistake. Now they knew she did have them and knew where they were.

"Where they are right now doesn't concern us. If we have you, then that lawyer friend of yours will bring them to us to save your life. He is the one who has them right? He won't let you die."

Hamad was slowly advancing toward her. Melanie screamed and ran toward the door, but he had anticipated that, and stepped in front of her. She turned and ran toward the fireplace. *If I can get the poker I can hit him over the head and get away.*

He was a big man and could easily overwhelm her. They circled the room, Melanie doing her best to stay away from him; Hamad laughing as he stalked her. Melanie deliberately overturned over one of the chairs by the fireplace hoping that would make it more difficult to get her, but it didn't make any difference.

She picked up the poker and swung it at Hamad's head. When he ducked, she ran toward the door, right into the arms of the second man. He was laughing.

"She led you on a merry chase Hamad, you must be getting old," he exclaimed

Taking two pieces of cord from his pocket Hamad said "hold her while I tie her up."

Melanie was screaming obscenities at them. "Let go of me right now." She was also doing her best to kick the man behind her.

"Feisty one isn't she?" the man behind her remarked, "Alex will enjoy having her in his bed."

Hamad leered into her face "Shut up, or we will both enjoy you here, and there is nothing you can do to stop us."

Melanie couldn't stop screaming, "Please don't hurt me?" she begged.

Hamad tied her hands and feet, and then taking a syringe from his pocket, jabbed it through her pants into her upper thigh. Inadvertently, he dropped the plastic cover of the needle to the floor. "I can't stand your screeching. My ears hurt from listening to you."

Within seconds Melanie felt her limbs get heavy and blackness overtake her. She slumped to the floor.

Hamad picked her up and slung her over his shoulder. "Let's get out of here."

He carried Melanie to the car, tossed her into the back seat, and then got into the front seat. The men drove to an airfield about half an hour from Farmington where a private jet was waiting for them.

Hamad removed the sleeping Melanie from the car, and carried her into the plane. He placed her into one of the seats, tightening the seat belt around her. Then he pushed a button on the seat until it was in a reclining position. Within minutes the pilot started the engines and was ready for takeoff

"What if she wakes up?"

"If she begins to stir, I will inject her again."

The plane took off and climbed into the blue sky.

Six hours later Melanie opened her eyes and tried to focus. "Where am I, and why am I here?" She managed to ask before she felt the prick of the needle in her arm. Darkness overcame her once more.

Chapter Eighteen

Suddenly, Adam had a strong feeling something was terribly wrong, but couldn't figure out where it was coming from. This was different than anything he had felt before. Then it hit him. Melanie – something had happened to her.

He cursed himself. Since they had put the last orb into the safe he had allowed his guard to relax. Other than the two strangers coming and leaving town, there seemed to be nothing to worry about.

Immediately, he pulled his cell phone from his shirt pocket and dialed Melanie's number, but there was no answer. *I know she was coming to town, so maybe she isn't home yet*. He paced his office, but the feeling of dread continued to build in his chest. He phoned every five minutes, the phone continued to ring in the empty house.

Finally, he couldn't stand the suspense any longer. He went out to his receptionist and said to her, "put off my appointments for the rest of the day," and then he was out the door.

"What should I say," she called behind him, but he was already out of hearing range.

He drove up and down every street in the business area of the town, but there was no sign of her old car. s He became more and more uneasy, the feeling that Melanie was in danger continued to get stronger.

What kind of trouble has she got herself into this time? he fumed, as he broke the speed limit driving to her place. As soon as he drove into the yard and approached the house, he saw the front door was open, and her car was in its usual parking spot. He bailed out of his car and ran through the front door.

"Melanie" he called out, but there was no answer "Melanie," he shouted louder, but still there was nothing.

He hurried to the kitchen. The peanut butter and jam were on the cupboard, her purse and car keys were lying on the table. Back tracking he went into the parlor – the sandwich and a cold cup of tea sat on the coffee table. One of the chairs by the fireplace was lying on its side, the fireplace utensils were scattered, and the room was in total disarray. *What on earth went on here?*

He ran up the stairs, but the doors of the three rooms were locked. He checked the cellar, the bed and bathroom. He checked the dining room and the library, but they appeared undisturbed

He hurried back into the parlor and, just beside the door frame he spotted the plastic cover used to protect the needle of a syringe.

"What the hell?" he cursed. Pulling his cell phone from his pocket, he called the police

"I need you to come out to Mattie's old farm. Something has happened out here."

While he was waiting, he noticed a piece of paper lying on the rug under the coffee table. Picking it up, he saw it was a note. 'We have her. Wait for instructions.'

Then it came to him. The two men had come back for the orbs. Did they know Melanie was a Seer? How long until they figured out that they needed both the Seer and the orbs?

When the police arrived they did a thorough search of the house and property. Adam took the police chief, Lou Duncan, into the parlor and showed him the syringe cover, as well as the note.

"Looks to me like this might be a kidnapping. Do you have any idea why, or what this could be about?"

Adam explained, carefully choosing his words, "Mattie had a secret she passed to her granddaughter."

"Do you know what the secret is Adam?" the police chief asked.

"Yes, but I'm not at liberty to say, but I think it's the reason she was kidnapped."

"What makes you think that?"

Adam explained about the two strangers approaching her in the grocery store, and then showing up at the house. "They were looking to buy three glass balls, and were willing to pay an exorbitant price for them. I have a feeling those are the guys who did this?"

"What can you tell me about them?'

"Not much, except that they were foreigners, and spoke with distinctive accents. One was called Hamad, or something like that. I didn't give them a chance to explain, just ran them off by threatening to call the police."

"I'll ask again. Do you know what the secret is?"

"Lawyer client privilege chief. I know that's not what you want to hear, but until Melanie tells me different, that's the way it is." Adam replied.

The police chief replied "then it looks like the next move is up to them. We'll have to wait for them to contact you. Leave everything as it is in case we have to treat this as a crime scene later. Lock the door, and then I guess all we can do now is wait to hear from somebody. Maybe she will show up. Maybe she went for a long walk. You can't file a missing person's report for another twenty-four hours. In the meantime, I'll have the guys watching for her. Sorry Adam, but we have to follow procedure."

Adam did as he was told, but as he was driving out of the yard, he felt sick to his stomach. He had let Melanie down by not paying attention, and now she was in danger. In the deepest part of his being, he knew he had also failed all those who came before him.

Chapter Nineteen

The plane touched down smoothly and taxied to a private hanger located at the far end of the airport. When they got off the plane, a long black limousine was waiting for them. Hamad carried the still sleeping Melanie to the limousine, propped her up in one of the corners, and then buckled her in.

The driver of the car drove through the streets until he came to the palace gates. Punching in a security code, he drove through the gates and around the back. A big burly servant removed Melanie out of the car, and carried her upstairs to a large bedroom. He laid her on the bed, double checked to make sure the windows were locked and left, locking the door behind him.

Hamad went into the study where General Alex was waiting for him, "good to see you back safely my friend. Did she give you any trouble?"

Hamad replied, "She tried, and it took both of us to finally subdue her. She has been sleeping for hours now, but should awaken shortly."

"What about that lawyer guy?"

"He will have no idea where she has gone. How long are you going to wait before you communicate with him?"

"Another day or so, I want to make sure she agrees to marry me first. After the ceremony is complete, and I have consummated the marriage, he can give the orbs to me as a wedding present.

I was thinking after you left. I will get her pregnant as soon as possible, and then when she has a daughter, I'll control the Seers for future generations. The orbs will never have to leave the palace."

"You seem to have it all figured out," Hamad replied, "but I warn you she is a feisty one. I doubt if she will cooperate with you."

"You know me Hamad, I can be very persuasive when I have to be. Where did you put her?"

"In the pink room, down the hall from your suite, I sent Melanah to sit with her until she awakes."

"Hamad, why don't you take a couple days, you deserve some time off for doing a good job. Help yourself to whomever and whatever you wish."

Hamad excused himself and backed out of the room. Alex sat there contemplating his triumph. His plan was going well. From now on he would be unstoppable, first the continent, and then the world.

Melanie struggled to open her eyes. Her arms and legs felt as heavy as lead, and her eyelids felt the same.

"You are finally awake," an accented female voice said to her," you must rest and let the drugs wear off."

"Where am I?" Melanie struggled to say. Her mouth was dry and her tongue felt thick.

"You are in Zahara."

"Where in the hell is Zahara?" Melanie mumbled, but fell asleep again before she heard the answer.

She drifted in and out of wakefulness for the next several hours. Each time she awoke the voice returned, "go back to sleep."

When she awoke this time she felt more alert. "Water please," she managed to get out. The woman held a plastic bottle of water to her lips and she drank her fill.

"Who are you?" she slurred.

"I am Melanah. I have been instructed to watch over you until you are fully awake."

Suddenly Melanie's eyes opened wide. The last thing she remembered was fighting with a man at home in her parlor.

She began to panic, "where am I?"

Her voice sounded hysterical even to herself. She tried to get off the bed "I have to get out of here, I need to call Adam."

"Please Melanie, try to relax. You are safe."

Melanie looked over to where the voice was coming from. A very beautiful young woman dressed in tan slacks and printed blouse was sitting in a chair beside her bed.

Melanie looked at her and began to cry, "Please help me. I don't know what's happening. I have to phone Adam and have him come get me."

"Hush now, go back to sleep."

"I have to go to the bathroom."

"Will you be able to walk, if I help you?"

"I think so."

Melanah helped Melanie off the bed, and supported her as they walked to the bathroom, located at the far end of the room

Before she called to Melanah to help her back, Melanie splashed her face with cold water and looked around. She had never seen a bathroom like this before.

The entire room was done in blue and green marble. There was a huge soaker tub and a shower with five nozzles. All of the fixtures were solid gold. A crystal chandelier hung from the ceiling. The floor length mirror was gilded in gold leaf.

There was a knock at the door, "are you ready to go back to bed Miss Melanie."

Before she opened the door Melanie looked in the mirror, barely recognizing the person staring back at her. There were deep blue circles under her eyes, and her hair was flying in all directions. She was still wearing the same clothes as the day before. *What's going on here? I don't understand.*

She stumbled to the door and opened it. Melanah helped her back to bed, and this time covered her with a light blanket. She drifted between sleep and wakefulness for several more hours.

The next time she woke up, her mind felt clearer. When she heard the voices of Hamad and Melanah, she pretended to still be asleep. She didn't want them to know she could hear them.

"How much longer will she sleep? Alex is getting impatient to meet her."

"She should soon be awake. How much did you give her? She should have been fully awake hours ago. You could have killed her."

When she does wake up you are to let Alex know immediately."

"I will Hamad. Go now. I know what I am doing."

When Melanie heard the door open and then close, she opened her eyes "May I have more water please?" she asked.

Melanie was a survivor. She had been looking after herself since her mother died. *My best tactic now was to find out why I have been brought here and where I am. I need to find out where the closest embassy is, and a way to get there.* She knew she would try to escape and make a run for it. Now that she had a plan, she felt calmer.

When Melanah handed her a bottle of water she drank half without stopping. "Thank you" she said, "Now please, tell me where I am, and how I got here?"

"You are in the Generals Palace in Zahara. He is the one responsible for bringing you here."

"Where is Zahara?"

"In Africa."

Melanie felt more confused than ever. "What does this General want from me?"

"You will meet him soon and find out for yourself. In the meantime, I have ordered some tea and food for you."

"I don't want it."

Melanah put her hand under Melanie's chin, turning her face to meet hers.

"Melanie, you must listen to me. General Alex is a very cruel man, and you should do your best not to make him angry. You have had no food for more than twenty-four hours. He prides himself on his hospitality, and will be very disappointed if you don't eat."

There was a knock at the door. Malanah opened it, and a young girl about ten years old came in bearing a tray with fresh fruit, bread, cheese and a large pot of tea.

"Thank you," Melanah said to her. The young girl smiled back and then turned and practically ran from the room.

"I will try to find you something to wear while you are eating," Melanah said.

Melanie heard the door lock from the outside after she left. She quickly got off the bed and hurried to the windows. Desperately she tried to open each one of them, but they were locked. Outside she saw she was in a walled compound and underneath her window was a circular driveway. *This must be the front of the house.. That should make it easier to escape if I can get out of this room..*

Realizing she was trapped, she went back to the tray. *I have to eat, so I can keep my strength up..* She nibbled on a piece of fruit and a slice of cheese, and forced herself to swallow half of the piece of bread. The tea was different than anything she had tasted before – a combination of lemon and orange flavors, and something else she couldn't quite place.

All too soon Melanah returned. "General Alex is waiting for you downstairs" she said. "I suggest you shower and get tidied before you meet him. I've brought you some clothes. I will send your clothes to the laundry, and have them returned to you."

Melanie got up and walked to the bathroom. She had a shower, washed her hair, and then put on the loose flowing blue dress, panties and sandals Melanah had brought. When she came out of the bathroom she said "I don't have a bra."

"General Alex doesn't want you to wear one. Come, he is waiting."

Melanie followed as Melanah led her through the hallway, down the long curving staircase, and into an office. Melanie felt like she was gawking, she had never seen so much opulence.

. When they entered the office, a very tall handsome man stood to greet her. His English was excellent, but the thing Melanie noticed was his blue eyes. They were hard and cruel. Even though he was smiling, the smile didn't reach his eyes

"Welcome to Zahara Miss Caine. I hope you have a most pleasant stay with us. Here sit down. Can I get you something to drink?"

"No, I am fine thank you."

The two adversaries stared at each other. Melanie was determined not to be the first to speak.

Finally Alex walked over to a tall window and stared outside. "I suppose you are wondering why I brought you here."

"You could say that," Melanie responded, trying to keep the tremor out of her voice

Then he turned and stared at her. "Are you afraid of me Miss Cain?"

"Should I be?"

Alex laughed, "That's up to you."

"What do you want from me? You didn't go to this much trouble to find out if I was afraid of you. I don't scare that easily."

"It's easy," he said, looking at her "I want you and the orbs."

"Why?"

"Isn't it obvious? With you and the orbs, I will eventually rule the world. You can use your abilities to show me the best tactics to use to accomplish my goal. You will marry me, and our daughter will be a Seer, and I will be in control of that too."

"Are you crazy or what? There is no way I will agree to something like that."

He smiled a wolf like smile. "I can be very persuasive. Now you will phone your lover and tell him to bring me the orbs.

"And if I refuse?"

He stalked over to her, clamped his hand on her breast and twisted. Tears came to her eyes. "This is just the beginning of what I can do to you. The rest will be far more unpleasant. I guarantee you will agree to speak to him just to make me stop hurting you."

Melanie stared back at him as if to say I can take anything you can hand out.

"I will give you time to come around to my way of thinking. You will convince your lover to give me the orbs as a wedding present."

"He is not my lover, he is my lawyer."

"Good, no sentimental attachment. That will make it easier for him to do as he is told."

Then calling Melanah back into the room, he said "Take her back to her room and try to talk some sense into her."

Melanie stood up, turned her back to him, and with her head held high and began to walk out. Then she turned and said "it will be a cold day in hell before I do anything for you." She could hear Alex's laughter follow her up the stairs as she walked back to her room.

Hamad told me she was a feisty one, and she definitely will be a challenge, but that doesn't matter. I always win one way or another. I have never been bested by a woman. Even the most spirited can be broken.

Melanah led her back to her room. Once the door was closed she said, "Don't stand up to him like that. He likes hurting people, especially women."

Several hours later Hamad let himself into Melanie's room. Although she appeared to be resting, she was frantically trying to figure out what to do next. She didn't know where she was, and didn't know to communicate with Adam.

"You, come with me. Alex wants to see you."

"I'm not going anywhere with you. I am staying here," Melanie replied, looking at him

Hamad grabbed her wrist and yanked her off the bed, "you will do as I say or I will shoot you."

Melanie laughed bitterly, "No you won't Hamad. We both know that I am of no use to you if I'm dead."

Straightening her shoulders, she walked in front of Hamad and she made her way back to Alex's office. When she entered the room, Alex picked up the phone and said, "Put my call through now."

Chapter Twenty

Adam was trying to sleep when his cell phone rang at three o'clock in the morning. Maybe this was the call they had been waiting for. He had convinced the police to place a tap on his phone and they were ready to trace where the call was coming from.

"Hello," he said, trying to sound sleepy, but he doubted his acting would fool anybody.

"Good morning Lawyer Brighton," Alex said

"It's three o'clock in the morning," Adam growled.

"I know what time it is there. I have somebody who wishes to speak to you." He handed the phone to Melanie.

"Adam," she said.

"Melanie? Are you hurt? Where are you, I have been so worried about you."

"I am fine – I haven't been hurt yet. Adam please listen to him, I need your help."

Alex snatched the phone from her hand. "You can see she is fine, now listen to me. You will get the orbs, and bring them to me. You will receive instruction soon. Follow them exactly. You should arrive in time to see me marry your girlfriend, and then you can give the orbs to us as a wedding present," he laughed cruelly. Handing the phone back to Melanie he said "now say goodbye."

"Do as he says Adam."

"Are you sure about this Melanie?"

"Yes."

Alex took the phone back. "I am getting tired of waiting Lawyer Brighton. She is a very tempting morsel, and I'm not going to wait very long before I begin to sample her sweetness. You do understand what I mean don't you?" Then the line went dead.

"Damn you," Adam shouted into his phone. "Don't you dare touch her."

Seconds later his cell phone rang again. "Did you get that?" he said to the voice on the other end.

"We traced the call to the city of Zahara in Africa. We are dealing with General Alex, the so-called ruler and leader of the rebel forces. How did she get mixed up with him?"

"They came for her. Now what are you going to do?"

"I'll contact our embassy there, and see if they have anyone available to help us. In the meantime, get the orbs and be ready to go.

"If he gets his hands on them, and has Melanie, this could be a very dangerous situation," Adam said, "He intends to rule the world."

"I will take your word for it Mr. Brighton. In the meantime you must be ready to do exactly what he says. Once you get there, be prepared for anything, and make sure your phone is in working order. Before you leave we should establish a code to alert you if some kind of action is going to take place, but at this point, I have no idea what it could be. We need to get the Embassy there to cooperate with us."

"He's on his way," Alex leered at Melanie. "Now I will tell you what is going to happen. You will marry me and produce a daughter. According to the ancient texts, she will be a Seer just as you are. When she is old enough, you will train her to read the orbs. I will be unstoppable."

"You are delusional. There is no way I'm going to go along with this."

"Dear sweet Melanie you have no choice in the matter. Now," he said, offering her his arm.
"it's time for supper, shall we go?"

Melanie couldn't resist getting the last word in. "I would rather die than marry you."

"And I can drug you and help myself; either way doesn't matter to me. Your lover can watch if that's preferable to you, but for now you will eat. You will need your strength to keep up with me."

All during the meal Alex asked Melanie questions, but she refused to answer him.

After the meal Alex sent for Melanah to take Melanie back to her room. "You must do as he asks," she said.

Melanie looked at her, "in my country it is called rape and forcible confinement."

"And here Alex can do whatever he wants. There is nobody to stop him, and nobody to help you."

When Melanah left she locked the door behind her. Melanie threw herself on the bed and cried. *What is going to happen now?*

Chapter Twenty One

Adam drove to his office. Entering through the back door he went to the safe and unlocked it. Rather than reaching for the crate he and Melanie had put in there, he pulled out an identical looking box; only this one was small enough to carry in his briefcase.

After Mattie and Simeon returned from Masada, Simeon had an identical looking set of the orbs made, exactly for this kind of situation. Only the Sentinels knew this secret, the Seer had never been told.

Adam knew Melanie would know the difference right away, but the General wouldn't. The problem was how was he going to tell Melanie?

He had no sooner locked the door to his office when his cell phone rang again. "There is an abandoned airstrip fourteen miles east of Colombo. Be there at noon, come alone and bring the orbs."

Minutes later his cell phone rang again. "Did you get that?" Adam asked.

"Yes we are dispatching men there now. We have been in contact with the embassy, and there is a plan in place. Do you have what you need?"

"Yes," Adam replied "I'm ready."

At eleven-fifty the next morning Adam was waiting at the airstrip. He parked his car, spoke to the unit leader of the police, and then settled down to wait. A few minutes after twelve, a private jet landed. When it came to a full stop, and the stairs were lowered, Adam walked into the plane carrying his briefcase.

A voice announced over the intercom, "Buckle up Mr. Brighton. There are drinks and food in the galley, help yourself. Our flight time is eight hours, so you might as well relax."

Minutes later the plane lifted off into the clear blue sky. At first Adam was apprehensive, but then he calmed down. Even if there was a plan in place, he had no idea how he was going to get Melanie out of there alive.

What Adam didn't know was that the local government had been looking for a reason to dispose of General Alex. Melanie and the orbs provided the excuse they needed. In fact, Melanie and Adam had now become pawns in a game being played by both sides. In the whole scheme of things their lives were of no value.

As Adam flew across the ocean, Alex was moving ahead with his marriage preparations. There would be no feast, no celebrations and as soon as the ceremony was over, and the orbs were in his hands, Hamad had instructions to kill Adam.

While Melanie was stricken and distraught over her lover's death, he would take her to the bedroom and force himself upon her. By then she would realize there was no way out and that her last chance of being saved was gone. She would be at his mercy. Once she became pregnant she would be confined to her room until the baby was born.

The child would be raised by a nurse. If the baby was a girl, Melanie would enjoy the same fate as all his other women – passed hand-to-hand to whoever wanted her starting with Hamad. If the child was a boy, she would be impregnated again as soon as she was able to conceive..

Alex explained his plans to Hamad. "I can barely wait to claim her little body; I have great plans for her."

"But Alex, this is about having her here to read the orbs for you, why go through all of this. You have other ways of making her talk and tell you what she sees."

"I want to have complete control over the mother, the daughter and the orbs. No one will be able to stop me. I will be invincible. If I have sons they will follow in my footsteps."

Hamad thought Alex was a little mad, but didn't say so. He was trying to figure out where he fit into this picture.

It was dark when Adam's plane landed. A black limousine was waiting and took him to the Palace. On the plane he handcuffed the briefcase containing the orbs to his wrist, and set a code for the lock. He was the only person who knew the combination..

Immediately, upon his arrival he was escorted to the General's office. Melanie was sitting on a chair beside the General.

"Good to see you have finally arrived Lawyer. Brighton. How nice of you to come for my wedding. I would like you to meet my wife-to-be Melanie Cain. I believe you two know each other?" He smiled maliciously. He reached over to Melanie and began fondling her breast. She gasped and cringed, trying to avoid his touch. Adam felt helpless.

Melanie looked at Adam, her eyes pleading for forgiveness. It went unsaid that if she had listened to him, they wouldn't be in this predicament.

Adam ignored Alex and walked over to her. Taking both of her hands in his he inquired, "Are you okay? Has he hurt you?"

"I am fine Adam, he hasn't touched me. This little show is for your benefit."

Alex chuckled, "after we are married tomorrow it won't matter what he thinks Melanie. You will be mine."

Then turning to Adam, he said "give me the orbs."

"No, not until I have had chance to speak to Melanie alone." Lifting his arm he said, "I'm the only one who knows the combination. You try to hurt me or her, and I could conveniently forget it. You don't scare me."

Alex chuckled again, "I see no harm in leaving you alone for short period of time, neither of you is going any place. When you are finished, I will have one of the servants escort you to your rooms. I have a set of twins waiting for me in my room. It's always interesting to spend an evening with them.

Turning to Hamad he said, "ten minutes, that's all. The lovers need a chance to say goodbye."

After both men left the room Melanie burst into tears. "I'm sorry Adam, and I am so scared."

He put his hands on her shoulders and looked into her eyes. "Listen to me. These people are very superstitious. If he asks you to read the orbs, feed his ego, make something up. Pull yourself together, and for once in your life do as I tell you." Quickly he explained about substituting the orbs.

"But he will know?"

"No, not if you don't let on. He has never seen them, therefore he doesn't know what they should look like.

There is also a faint possibility there will be a rescue attempt by government forces. If you see me answer my phone, or hear me say the words "what happened" be prepared for anything. Now go like a good girl and do what you are told, I don't think much is going to happen until tomorrow."

"Adam," Melanie begged, "Please forgive me for being so stupid. If you don't get out, or if I don't get out of here, I want you to know I love you."

Adam replied huskily "I love you too Melanie, and once we get out of here, I plan to show you how much."

Seconds later Hamad opened the door, "time is up."

Reluctantly they followed him up the stairs to their rooms.

Chapter Twenty Two

Melanah woke Melanie early the next the morning. "Get dressed. The General is downstairs waiting for you. Later we will come back to prepare for your wedding."

When Melanie entered the office, Adam and Alex were both waiting for her. Adam had shaved and dressed in white shirt and tan pants, and was sporting a black eye. The General also looked a little worse for wear. His eyes were bloodshot, and he was wearing the same clothes as the day before. Adam's briefcase, containing the orbs, sat on a nearby table

"Good morning Melanie" Alex said. "I have persuaded Adam to give us the orbs. Although he was reluctant to come around to our way of thinking, you can see that he changed his mind."

"Now I want to find out exactly what I have." Pointing to Adam, he demanded, "Unlock it." Adam limped across the room, and using the combination, reluctantly opened his briefcase and took out the box containing the orbs.

Melanie gasped when the box was opened. They looked exactly the same as the ones she had found. She looked at Adam with questions in her eyes, but his face didn't change, nor did he look at her. She could see that he was seething with anger.

Alex walked over, and in turn picked each one up turning it round and round in his hands. "This is what all this fuss is about? They don't look like anything special to me."

Adam responded, "To us, they are nothing, they can only be read by a Seer."

"Come here," he motioned to Melanie "tell me what they say."

"You have to ask a question first in order to get an answer," she replied sarcastically. Adam was right; General Alex had no idea oft the power he held in his hands.

He thought for a few minutes, and then asked, "How long shall I be the ruler of this country?"

Melanie glanced at Adam, and then made a show of moving the orbs to various positions.

"What does it say?" Alex demanded to know.

"It reads, "As it is now, so it shall be unto the end.""

"What does that mean?" Alex roared "that is nonsense."

Melanie turned pale. "I don't know what it means. You have to interpret and discern the meaning for yourself. To me it clearly means you are the ruler now, and will continue to be so until the end. You may die as the ruler or be overthrown; I have no way of knowing. I can only tell you what the orbs say to me, the rest you have to figure out for yourself."

"Try this one – are all who reside within my palace loyal to me?"

Melanie repeated her actions with the orbs. "We all have enemies we count as friends. Choose carefully."

Adam smiled, and relaxed a little. *Melanie is good at this.*

Then Alex asked "try this one, when we are married will we be blessed with a daughter?"

"No" Melanie replied, without consulting the orbs, "because I refuse to marry you."

He grabbed her by the hair and yanked. Melanie cried out in surprise.

Adam jumped off his chair. "Take your hands off her."

Hamad, who had been standing behind Adam all this time, grabbed his shoulders and forced him back into the chair.

"Hamad, go tell Melanah to prepare her for our marriage ceremony." To Adam he said coldly "you will watch as I force your girlfriend to give in to me, and then I have instructed Hamad to shoot you in front of her."

Adam lunged again, but Hamad hit him on the back of the head. Adam went down. Melanie screamed and fainted.

When she came to, she was once again lying on the bed. Melanah looked at her, "you must stop fighting him. He has made up his mind, and nothing will stop him. He will rape you every day until you get pregnant. The more you fight, the worse he will be."

"What happened to Adam?"

"He is fine, but he will have a headache for a while. I think he is downstairs having a drink with Alex. He realizes now that Alex can't be stopped. Come, we must get you ready."

Reluctantly Melanie went through the motions. She prayed Adam's call would come to her rescue before it was too late.

Melanah helped her dress, and then did her hair, intertwining flowers within the curls. Her dress was made of a sheer, white, gauze like material.

"I refuse to wear this," Melanie said, "you can see right through it."

Suddenly Melanah snapped at her "just put it on and stop whining. You are in our country now, and this is what General Alex wants. I am tired of listening to you. The wedding is at two, and we dare not be late."

Melanie was puzzled by Melanah's change of attitude. "I am sorry," she apologized, "this isn't exactly what I had planned for my wedding day."

Melanie put on the dress, and then twirled in circles. "How do I look?" she asked.

Melanah looked at her watch. "General Alex will be pleased. Come, we have to go now. The wedding is to take place in the garden."

Melanie shuddered as they walked down the hallway to the garden. *I will do whatever is asked of me, but the first chance I get I will escape.*

The sun was shining, and it was a hot humid day. Once in a while Melanie felt a cool breeze brush her hot cheeks. She looked at Adam, but he stared straight ahead, his eyes not betraying his thoughts.

Alex had changed, and was dressed in his General's uniform. There was a gun at his side. Adam, Hamad and Melanah were the only guests. A table, with bottles of champagne cooling in buckets of ice, sat off to one side.

Soon an older man wearing a white clerical collar hurried into the garden. "Sorry I am late, the natives are restless today." He chuckled at his own joke. "Are you ready General?"

Melanie stood off to one side, her eyes imploring Adam to do something, but he continued looking straight ahead.

Alex walked to her side and took her hand. "You look lovely," he said. "I phoned your Embassy and requested a Christian minister so you would feel more comfortable. You may start now," he said to the minister. Melanie felt as though her world was coming to an end.

Just as the minister began the ceremony, Adam's cell phone rang. Alex scowled at the interruption. Adam listened to the caller, and then shouted "never mind that, tell me what happened."

Suddenly there was shooting in the palace yard. The sound of gun fire and loud shouting was heard coming from the street. Soldiers were running every which way.

"What is going on here," Alex shouted. Then he realized. "We are being attacked by government forces."

He pulled out his pistol and pointed it at Adam. "You" he stuttered. More shots rang out, and Hamad fell to the ground.

The minister grabbed Melanie's arm and began dragging her toward the gate. "You need to come with me."

When she looked back she spotted Adam struggling with Alex.

The minister said "we must get through the front gate, hurry."

A shot rang out behind her, but Melanie kept running. Outside the gate, a private car was waiting. The minister pushed her in, and climbed in behind her. The car sped off. Ten minutes later it pulled into the Embassy gates.

"What about Adam?"

"They will try to bring him out safely. Our mission was to capture or kill General Alex."

Melanie was hurried into the Embassy and led into a large office. The man took off his clerical collar, "may I get you something to drink while we are waiting," he asked casually.

Melanie turned on him, "you used us."

"You might say that my dear. We have been looking for an opportunity to get rid of General Alex for a long time. You and your friend provided the distraction we needed."

"What about Adam?"

"We will have to wait and hear what happens to him. We have a person in place who is to see he gets away unharmed, but I cannot guarantee his safe return."

Melanie heard shouting, gunfire, and the scream of sirens far into the night. She paced back and forth, jumping at every new sound. Then the office door opened and Adam stumbled in followed by Melanah. There was blood on Adam's shirt and face. Malanah was limping

"Adam," Melanie cried out, running to him. "You are covered with blood, are you hurt?" She threw her arms around him, and began kissing his face.

"No, this is General Alex's blood. Melanah shot him in the head while we were struggling over his gun. Then we had a hard time getting away from the palace without being shot. We got here by sneaking up and down back alleys."

An aide to the Ambassador knocked, and entered the room, "We have confirmation that General Alex has been killed sir."

Melanie turned and stared at Melanah. "You knew all the time."

"Yes, he deserved what he got, and then some," she replied, and then said no more.

"You best stay here for now," the Ambassador said, "We will try to get you home tomorrow. Melanah will be returning with you, she hasn't seen her family for a very long time."

None of them seemed to want to leave the others. It was as though they were on an island, and as long as they stayed together, they were safe. Adam and Melanie sat close together on the sofa holding hands. Melanah sat on a comfortable chair with her swollen ankle propped up on a footstool. The Ambassador sat behind his desk.

Every once in a while the Ambassador's phone rang, and he received an update on what was happening.

"Excuse me," he said at one point, and left the room. He returned some time later, pushing a cart with tea, coffee and a tray filled with sandwiches. Folded across his arm was a faded blue bathrobe.

"Excuse me Miss Cain, but that dress is extremely revealing. I thought perhaps you would feel more comfortable wearing this," he said, handing her the robe. "I had the cook make us something to eat, so I hope you are hungry."

Melanie accepted it, but his comment broke the tension in the room. Her face turned bright red as she stood and put on the robe, wrapping it tightly around her.

The next time the phone rang the Ambassador smiled. "Good news, our forces have regained control of the palace, police station, government offices and the airport. The raid at the rebel camp was also successful. We caught them by surprise."

"I have arranged for rooms upstairs. Anytime you wish to retire, one of the staff will take you to your room.

Suddenly Melanie felt exhausted, so tired she could barely function. The day's events were rapidly overwhelming her. At the same time the Ambassador looked over his guests and noticed how tired they all looked.

"All of you should go up to your rooms and get some rest. The Embassy is heavily guarded so you are safe. In the morning, which is not that far away, you will need to be debriefed and asked to make an official statement. By then we should be able to get a doctor to look at your ankle Melanah. Can you bear the pain until then?"

She nodded yes.

Adam was lying awake unable to sleep, trying to make sense of events of the last thirty six hours. There was a soft knock on his door, and then he heard it open. Instantly he was alert.

"Adam, are you awake," Melanie whispered, "can I come in?"

"Yes," he replied.

She came and stood by the side of his bed. "I'm afraid. Please hold me."

"Come here," he replied gruffly. He pulled back the covers and she lay down beside him. She was trembling. She curled her body around him, her head on his chest. He wrapped one arm around her shoulders, and held the hand on his chest with the other. Soon Melanie's trembling ceased, her breathing became soft and regular, and they both slept. Adam's last thought before sleep overtook him was *now is not the time for us to deal with our feelings for each other.*

Chapter Twenty Three

When Adam awoke the next morning Melanie was gone. He got up, showered, and when he came out of the bathroom he found his clothes freshly laundered and pressed, waiting for him. His first concern was for Melanie.

As he walked past her room, he saw the door was open and the room was empty. He hurried down the stairs and followed the voices coming from a room across the hall. Melanie, the Ambassador, and two other men were sitting at the table having breakfast. Adam noticed Melanie was wearing a white T-shirt, and a pair of jeans rolled up because they were too long for her. She looked rested.

"Adam," the Ambassador greeted him. "We are just having breakfast, come join us."

Melanie looked up at him shyly

"This is General Alonso and General Brett. They led the government forces last night. They wish to ask both of you some questions about how you came to be here."

When they finished eating, they moved to the Ambassador's office. A secretary was called in, and Melanie and Adam each gave their statement.

"We will have it ready for you to sign within the next few hours, after that you are free to go."

The Generals and Ambassador had difficulty believing their story but, since there was no other explanation, they had to accept it.

"I once heard of such a thing many years ago," General Alonso said, "it is a story told by the old scribes. The orbs, where are they?"

"The originals are at still at home locked in my safe. This is a fake set I brought with me. There has always been a contingency plan just in case something like this should happen."

"General Alex didn't know the difference?"

"He didn't know what to expect in the first place. He had loftier ambitions. The orbs and kidnapping Melanie were merely a means to an end."

"You have done our country a great service," General Alonso said. "I thank you."

"I do have one question," Adam asked, "I've been thinking this over, and I keep coming back to the same question. Were Melanie and I expendable?"

"Yes, to be honest with you. Your presence gave us an excuse to move our plans forward. Of course we wanted you to be safe, but that wasn't our primary goal. General Alex was a dictator and we needed to get rid of him. You," he said looking at Melanie "provided a worthwhile distraction for him. He's always had a soft spot for a beautiful woman."

"What about Melanah?"

"Hamad recruited her to work in the Palace, and then abused her very badly. She barely survived. After she recovered from her injuries, she came to us and volunteered to bring us information. Originally a student from your country, she came to help the women who were suffering under General Alex's regime. Unwillingly she found herself victimized by the palace officials. It is a long story, but is hers to tell.

Melanie, when she heard you had been kidnapped and brought to the palace, she volunteered to stay with you, putting her own life at great risk.

Last night we captured one of General Alex's private jets at the airport. Once it has been checked over you will be flown home."

Hours later Melanie, Adam, and Melanah in the air, their pilot handpicked by the Ambassador's staff.

The trip was quiet. Melanie and Melanah slept most of the way. Adam stared out the window. *How am I going to explain to Melanie that now we have to go our separate ways? I'm not sure I even want to?*

Chapter Twenty Four

Police Chief Lou Duncan was waiting for Adam and Melanie when their plane landed. Melanah was met and whisked away by several men in an official looking car.

"Wait for me in the car Melanie. I'll see what he wants." Then turning to the police chief he asked "what can I do for you Lou?"

"We need a statement from Miss Cain, regarding what took place in her home. After that it will be case closed."

"Not today Lou okay. She has been through a very difficult time and is exhausted. Will tomorrow be good enough? Will she need a lawyer with her?"

"No problem Adam. We have a few questions and that's all. Tell her I will be there sometime after lunch."

While Adam was talking to the police Melanie got into his car, put her head back and closed her eyes. *What happened to my neat orderly life? Ever since I came here it has been like a roller coaster ride. I didn't ask for any of this, and I know Adam is furious with me, and I don't blame him.*

Adam was quiet as he drove Melanie home. Neither of them knew what to say to the other. They had avoided all personal discussion and contact since leaving Zahara.

When they drove into the yard Adam said, "You stay in the car while I check things out. I don't want to walk into any surprises."

Melanie did as she was told, and a few minutes later she saw him waving at her from the front step. Leading her into the parlor he said, "Lou Duncan is going to come by after lunch tomorrow to get a statement from you." He hesitated for several seconds, and then said, "We need to talk Melanie."

"Don't you think it would be better to do this another time? We are both tired."

"No, what I have to say can't wait. Come and sit down."

Once they were seated across from each other Melanie said, "I'm sorry Adam. I didn't mean for any of this to happen.

"That's the problem Melanie, I asked you to leave this alone. I hoped you would go back home and stay there. I knew what would happen once you had all of the orbs."

"I don't understand, what you're talking about?"

"Melanie I can't do this. I am in love with you, but as your Sentinel, I can't let my feelings get in the way. My role is to protect you, and I can't allow my feelings for you stop me from doing my job. I have to make a choice.

If we get romantically involved, the lines of Sentinel and Seer will end with us, plus we will be breaking one of the cardinal rules. Any children we might have will not inherit our abilities. If we don't, then I don't know how we can live separate lives. It will be impossible to see each other only as friends. What right do we have to decide for future generations? That's what we will be doing if we are selfish and put our own feelings first. You tell me what the right answer is?"

Adam was pacing back and forth, running his fingers through his hair. He would stop, stare at Melanie, and then shake his head. "I nearly lost you. This isn't about what you or I want. This is about doing fulfilling my duty to both the past, and the future Sentinels. I am responsible for you"

Melanie sat quietly watching him pace and then replied, her voice beginning to rise. "That's your biggest problem Adam. Everything you do has to be done by the book – things are either right or wrong, and there is no middle ground. The one thing wrong with this picture is that you haven't asked me what I want."

"What's that?" Adam demanded, his frustration coming through in his words. He stopped pacing and looked at her, "you are right I haven't. What do you want?"

"I want my life back. I was happy before I knew all of this. I had a purpose for living and a focus. I don't care about being a Seer. It means nothing to me. In fact, it has cost me years of unhappiness because I wasn't able to live with my grandmother. I don't want to live my life being afraid. I don't want or need your protection. I don't want you to feel responsible for me."

Sweeping her hand around the room she added, "I didn't ask for any of this. I came to my grandmother's funeral. I came to say good bye to my only living relative. I said I love you and I do. I fell in love with the man Adam Brighton, not a Sentinel who feels obligated to me. The way I see this is you are the one who has the problem."

"I can't do this." Adam said, getting to his feet and walking to the front door. "We can't do this," he added

"Well I guess that means you have made your choice, your antiquated sense of duty over me. There's the door, use it. I will look after myself from now on, just as I always have

Adam walked through the door slamming it closed behind him. Melanie watched as he drove away. The tears ran down her face. *I guess what I want isn't important.*

***.

Adam looked up from his desk as the town mayor entered his office. "Jack good to see you. What can I do for you today?"

"I need some information. You know how the town always wanted to buy Mattie Allen's place?"

"Yes."

"Miss Caine, who apparently is the new owner, approached us the other day about buying the place."

"She did? I had no idea she was thinking along those lines."

"Yeah, she offered to sell to us at a pretty decent price, but the question we have is about Mattie's will. Has it been probated and finalized? Not that we don't think she is within her rights, but before we go ahead, we want to be sure."

Adam was stunned. "You said she came to you a couple of days ago?"

"Yeah, said she was moving back to the city. She talked about using the money to buy a Florist shop."

"I'll have to get back to you on this Jack. I'm positive everything has been transferred to her, but I will check it out. How much is she asking?"

"Fifty thousand pounds."

"No wonder town council wants to buy her place. You and I both know it's worth at least three times that much."

"She did have one stipulation. The yard site and the house are to be used as a museum. She is willing to leave the antiques in the house for that reason."

Adam stood up and abruptly ushered the mayor to the door. They shook hands and Adam said "I will get on this right away."

Mattie what are you doing? You can't leave like this, I won't let you.

As soon as the Mayor was gone Adam snatched his jacket from the back of the chair "I'm going out to Mattie Allen's place," he called out to his receptionist, "If I have any more appointments cancel them."

When he arrived at Melanie's house he was glad to see her old car parked there. Angrily he marched up the front step and began pounding on the door.

"Melanie Caine, you open this door right now. Do you hear me?"

The door opened and Melanie stood there, her hands on her hips. ""To what do I owe this pleasure," she said sarcastically.

"What do you think you are doing offering the town this land and the antiques in the house for only fifty thousand pounds? It's worth at least three times that much."

"It's none of your business Adam. You have no right coming here to tell me what I can or cannot do. You chose what you wanted, now leave me alone."

"It is my business whether you like it or not. I am your Sentinel, your protector…"

By now Melanie was openly crying. "You just don't see it, do you. I can't stay here, it hurts too much."

"What are you saying?"

"I love Adam Brighton, the man, but I don't want anything to do with this part of him. I want him to love me for who I am, not because he feels obligated to keep me safe. Go home Adam. I need to do this."

"When are you leaving?"

"Day after tomorrow."

"Were you going to tell me?"

"No. Goodbye Adam," and she closed the door.

He was stunned by the sadness in her eyes and finality in her voice. As he stood there, he could hear her sobbing on the other side of the door.

In that moment he realized that if he walked away, and let her go, she would be out of his life forever. He started pounding on the door again.

"Open this door Melanie or I will break it down."

She opened it and looked at him.

"Marry me?"

"What?"

"I can't let you leave. Marry me."

"What about the Sentinel and all that stuff?"

"I choose you. The rest we will work out later." Then he stopped talking and looked at her, waiting for her answer.

"Yes," she said throwing her arms around him.

Epilogue

One year later Adam, and his wife Melanie, stood at the back of their rented boat and looked out over the ocean. Melanie held a wooden crate in her arms. Adam had one arm around her shoulders holding her close to his side. The other was placed on her bulging tummy. He felt the baby kick.

"It's time," he said.

Melanie reached over the railing and dropped the crate into the water. They stood there watching as it sank into the depths below. Neither said a word.

* * *

Far away the Ancient One smiled. "Eros, it has finally ended."

Eros heard him, smiled, and then commented, "At last. It should never have gone this far. Once again, the world is safe from this particular threat."

Then the Ancient One heard Eros say "well done my good and faithful servant, well done."

About the Author

Judy began writing after she retired from the business world. She viewed this as the opportunity to accept a new challenge in her life. The mother of four, and the grandmother of four boys, she lives in Alberta with her husband Bob and the Shitzu Missy Sue. Each November she joins NaNoWriMo in an attempt to write 50,000 words in 30 days. This encourages her to slip her creative boundaries and try something new.